Also by Ann M. Martin

Read more about Pearl Littlefield, her family, and her friends!

TEN GOOD and BAD things About MY LiFE (So far)

Ann M. Martin

FEIWEL AND FRIENDS

New York

A FEIWEL AND FRIENDS BOOK
An Imprint of Macmillan

TEN GOOD AND BAD THINGS ABOUT MY LIFE (SO FAR). Copyright © 2012 by
Ann M. Martin. All rights reserved. Printed in the United States of America by
R. R. Donnelley & Sons Company, Harrisonburg, Virginia. For information,
address Feiwel and Friends, 175 Fifth Avenue, New York, N.Y. 10010.

Library of Congress Cataloging-in-Publication Data Available

ISBN: 978-0-312-64299-0

Book design by Elizabeth Tardiff

Feiwel and Friends logo designed by Filomena Tuosto

First Edition: 2012

10 9 8 7 6 5 4 3 2 1

mackids.com

For Sarah and Cooper McGrath

"Lexie?" I said on the first day of fifth grade. "Are you nervous about school?"

It was 6:10 a.m., and I was in the hall outside my big sister's bedroom, leaning backward against her door, talking largely to the air. Lexie used to hang a NO PEARL sign on the door to keep me out, but these days I was welcome in her room as long as I was (a) fully clothed, since Lexie still didn't approve of underwear visits, and (b) prepared to start a meaningful conversation. Like, I couldn't interrupt her homework or her violin practice to say, "If Bitey died and then came back to life as a human, do you think he would ask me to marry him?" (Bitey is our cat.) Or, "Have you kissed your new boy-friend yet?" Actually, I thought the kissing question could start a very meaningful conversation, but Lexie never seemed to want to discuss either her boyfriend or kissing with me.

There was no answer from within Lexie's room. In fact, there was no sound at all in our apartment. That was probably because it was 6:10 a.m. Everyone was still asleep. Everyone except me, Pearl Littlefield. I was nervous about starting fifth grade. And I was curious to find out whether Lexie was nervous about starting high school.

"Lexie?" I said again. "Lexie?"

I heard a thump from my parents' room and decided to lower my voice.

"Lexie?" I said in a loud whisper.

"Pearl, WHAT?" replied my sister suddenly, yanking her door open. I fell into her room and landed on my bottom. "What are you doing? It isn't even six fifteen yet."

I got to my feet. "Are you nervous about school?"

Lexie clapped her hand to her forehead and flung herself on her bed. "You're asking me this now?"

Well, duh. It was the first day of school. When was I supposed to ask? "I need to know," I told her.

Lexie rolled her eyes. Or at least I think she did. She'd already closed her lids, but I could see that her eyeballs were rolling around underneath. "I guess so," she replied finally. "Everyone is nervous on the first day of school, Pearl."

2

"No, not everyone. I don't think JBThree is nervous."

JBIII is my new best friend. His complete name is James Brubaker the Third, but I shortened it to JBIII, which when you say it out loud it's JBThree.

"So maybe you should talk to JBThree," said Lexie, "and let me go back to sleep."

Her alarm rang then and she made a face at me, but frankly, it wasn't as mean a face as she would have made a few months ago. She turned off the alarm, patted me on the shoulder as she headed for the bathroom, and said, "You'll be fine, Pearl."

An hour and a half later I called good-bye to Mom and rode to the lobby of our apartment building with my father and Lexie and Lexie's cell phone. There's no cell-phone reception on elevators, but my sister had gotten a head start on her phone call by already speed-dialing her best friend Valerie's number. Now her thumb was poised over the Send button, prepared to press it the very second she stepped out of the elevator, so as not to waste a moment contacting Valerie about important high school business. But she didn't have to do that. When the elevator doors opened there were Valerie and also the two Emmas sitting on the couch in the lobby across from John, my favorite doorman. They were wearing a lot of black eyeliner and staring at their cell phones and not talking. But when they saw Lexie they jumped up, and the four of them started squealing and hugging like they hadn't just been together the afternoon before.

"Bye, Dad! Bye, Pearl!" called Lexie, and she and her grown-up high school friends rushed out the door and onto Twelfth Street.

When you're fourteen you don't need an adult to take you to school, even if you live in New York City. When you're ten you do. Also, just so you know, when you're fourteen you get to have a cell phone and your own personal computer. When you're ten, you don't. (Well, I don't.)

Dad and I walked past John, who gave me a high five and said, "Break a leg, Pearl," which is a nice thing to say, not a mean one, except you're supposed to say it to actors not students, but whatever.

We stepped outside and I looked across Twelfth Street, and there was JBIII coming out of his building with his mother who wanted to take a first-day-of-school picture. JBIII posed for one half of one second, and then joined Dad and me for the walk to Emily Dickinson Elementary.

"Remember the first day of school last year?" I said to my father. "You walked Justine and me to Emily Dickinson. This year you're walking JBThree and me."

"Things certainly do change," replied Dad, and I thought he looked a little sad. That was because there had been a lot of changes in our lives besides who I walked to school with.

We turned the corner onto Sixth Avenue and passed by all the familiar places in our neighborhood: New World, which is a coffee shop, and Steve-Dan's, which is my all-time favorite store because it sells art supplies, and Cuppa Joe, which is a new coffee shop, and Universal, which is a dry cleaner, and the Daily Grind, which is *another* new coffee shop. Over the summer Lexie and her friends started going to the Daily Grind to order Mocha Moxies, which they say are coffee drinks but which really look like giant milk shakes. Whenever Lexie starts talking about how she's grown-up enough to drink coffee what I want to say back to her is, "Mom and Dad don't squirt a tower of whipped cream on top of their coffee," but one thing I have learned lately is when not to say something.

When Dad and JBIII and I passed Monk's, which is a gift store, I could feel JBIII's eyes on me. Well, not actually *on* me, which would be gross, but suddenly I could tell he was looking at me and I knew why. We were now one half of a block away from Emily Dickinson, and JBIII and I had decided that no matter what anyone thought, we were simply too old to be walked right up to the door of our school by a parent.

"Dad," I said, "JBThree and I are ten years old now." (JBIII was actually a lot closer to eleven, while I was just barely ten.)

"Yes, you are," agreed Dad.

"And we think that—" JBIII frowned fiercely at me and I tried to remember the exact speech he had made me memorize the day before. "I mean," I said, backing up, "and we feel strongly that we should be allowed"—JBIII poked my arm—"that, um, we're responsible enough to walk the rest of the way to school by ourselves. Every day."

"You can stand here and watch us," said JBIII. And then he added quickly, "Sir."

"Well . . . ," said my father.

Dad has let me do this 2x before, but now JBIII and I were asking to do it regularly, and my father has a teensy problem with change, whether it's good or bad.

"*Please?*" I said, and now JBIII glared at me. He had also warned me not to whine. "Please, Father?" I said calmly.

"I suppose so."

"Yes!" I exclaimed.

"Thank you, sir," said JBIII.

"But remember—I'll be watching you."

"I know," I said. "Don't kiss me," I added, and JBIII and I ran down the block. Just before we reached Emily Dickinson I waved backward over my shoulder to Dad.

JBIII and I wound our way through the halls of Emily Dickinson. We passed by the first-grade room that Justine Lebarro had been in the year before, and then we passed

6

our old fourth-grade room. There was Mr. Potter, our teacher from last year, talking to his new students.

We kept on walking until we came to room 5A. I peeked through the doorway, then stepped back and flattened myself against the wall like a spy. "She's in there," I whispered to JBIII. "Ms. Brody."

Our teacher was new to Emily Dickinson. All we knew about her was her name.

JBIII peeked in, too. "She looks all right," he whispered to me.

The truth was that she looked very, very young, like if you switched her pants and her shirt for a white dress and a veil she could be a bride. I kept that thought to myself, though, because I could just hear Lexie clucking her tongue and saying to me, "A person can get married at any age, Pearl." But still in my head all brides were young.

"Afraid to go in?" said a voice from behind JBIII and me, and we both jumped.

I turned around to see Jill DiNunzio, who is a person I could live without.

"No," I said, doing an eye roll.

"So what are you waiting for?" she asked.

"Well, not you. Come on, JBThree."

JBIII and I marched into our new classroom, leaving Jill behind.

Fifth grade had officially begun.

Ms. Brody let us sit wherever we wanted, at least to begin with. So JBIII and I chose seats together in the last row. I had always wanted to have a best friend to sit with on the first day of school. And it was a relief not to wind up sitting directly in front of the teacher's desk like I did in Mr. Potter's room so he could keep an eye on me.

I watched Jill look around and take a seat by the window. I expected her to save seats for Rachel and Katie, but before I knew what had happened, Ms. Brody had closed the door to our room and said, "Welcome, fifth graders."

I raised my eyebrows. All the seats were taken.

Jill-Rachel-Katie had been split up. I almost jumped out of my chair and cried, "Yes!" but adults don't usually like that sort of thing and I wanted to make a good impression on Ms. Brody so she wouldn't be too mad the first time I left my homework papers under my bed or ran out of steam on a vocab assignment. (I am not a big fan of vocab.)

Ms. Brody began to talk about the things we would be studying in fifth grade, so I turned my attention to Jill and how she probably wouldn't be able to wield any power in our classroom all by herself. By the look of things, she didn't have any close friends at all in room 5A. And I had JBIII.

I could tell it was going to be a good year.

Next I thought about Lexie being in high school. I wondered what she and Valerie and the Emmas were doing right at that exact second. Then I thought about Bitey for a while, and then my parents, and finally I heard the word "homework."

Homework? Really? On the very first day of school? This seemed unfair.

"I want you to write an essay about your summer vacation," Ms. Brody was saying. "Please outline what you're going to write about, and then write from the outline."

Hmm. I thought that over. How would Ms. Brody know whether we had written an outline? I could probably skip that step.

"And please hand in both the outline and your essay tomorrow," Ms. Brody finished up.

I glanced at JBIII, all prepared to make a face about the awfulness of fifth grade, but he was taking notes on practically every word Ms. Brody said, since one thing he always does is every single assignment.

When school finally ended and JBIII and I were walking home ten steps ahead of my father (I didn't want to be rude, but really, it wasn't as if I hadn't walked the route to and from Emily Dickinson about 900x in my life), JBIII said to me, "Our essays are going to be pretty long, Pearl."

"I guess." I didn't want to think about homework just then.

"Let's go to your apartment and start them right now. We have a lot to write about."

I wanted JBIII to come over, but I did not want to start my homework. "Let's draw," I said to him, thinking longingly of my art supplies.

"Nope," said JBIII, but not in a mean way. "I want to do a good job on our first assignment for Ms. Brody."

"All right," I said at last.

As soon as we'd eaten a snack of apples and cheese sticks, JBIII and I sat down side by side on the floor of my bedroom. In the old days we would have settled in the family room, which is really the family room, living room, and dining room all in the same space. But recently the family room had become my father's office and he was sitting there now, glaring at his computer screen.

"Now," said JBIII in a businesslike voice, a pad of paper propped against his knees, "first things first." In his neatest printing he wrote M Y SUMMER VACATION— OUTLINE across the top of the first sheet of paper. He moved his pencil to the line below. "One," he said aloud, and wrote a Roman numeral one.

Oh, yeah. You're supposed to use Roman numerals on an outline. An interesting thing about Roman numerals is that JBIII has one in his name. III=3 in regular numbers.

I watched JBIII scratch busily away, making notes

about his summer, and I tried to remember how Roman numerals go. Then I thought for a while about Rome, which made me remember an exhibit on Rome that had been at the Museum of Natural History on one of the worst days of my life. It was the end of third grade and our class had taken a field trip to the museum and suddenly I couldn't find my classmates, only dinosaur skeletons, so I shouted, "Help! Police!" and got quite a few adults, including Mrs. DiNunzio (Jill's mother) and our teacher, in trouble for losing me. After that, the other third graders would whisper "Help! Police!" in my ear whenever they wanted to annoy me, which was pretty often, since they already thought I was a big baby. The incident at the museum might not have been so bad if there hadn't been two other incidents that year, one involving Show and Tell (which how was I supposed to know you don't have Show and Tell anymore when you get to third grade in Emily Dickinson Elementary?) and one involving my tinkle. Yes, there was an accidental wetting of my pants, but I don't want to go into the embarrassing details here. All you really need to know is that the whole year was embarrassing and that Jill and Rachel and Katie thought that every bad thing that happened to me was hilarious. Then we all turned up together in the same fourth-grade class, but by the end of that year JBIII and I had become friends, so I didn't care so much about Jill-Rachel-Katie.

"Pearl?" said JBIII.

"Yeah?"

"Aren't you going to start your outline?"

I looked at JBIII's paper, which was all spotted with Roman numerals and notes to himself. Then I looked at mine, which was blank.

"I'm still collecting my thoughts," I told him, and luckily at that moment, JBIII's mother phoned because she wanted him to come home.

When he left, I sat down at the desk and opened my notebook. After a very long time I wrote MY SUMMER VACATION—OUTLINE across the top, and then I made a capital letter I on the next line, which is how you write a Roman numeral one.

I stared and stared at the I, and at last I turned to a clean page in my notebook. What would be much, much more fun than writing an outline would be making questionnaires for my parents to fill out at dinnertime. I wrote Mom's in pink ink and Dad's in green:

Name _____

Age _____

Address _____

_____

Telephone numbers:

    Home _____

    Cell _____

Interests _____

_____

_____

Home: good _____ bad _____

Has husband or husband and children:

    yes _____ no _____

Likes cats: yes _____ no _____

Loves her family dearly: yes _____ no _____

This was Mom's questionnaire. I made a similar one for my father.

Then I settled down to start my outline. Next to the Roman numeral II wrote: My dad got fired.

MY SUMMER VACATION—OUTLINE

I. My dad got fired. (Sorry, Ms. Brody, but he didn't get ~~fried~~ fired over the summer, even though you asked about what happened on our vacations. He got fired before the summer. But almost everything that I'm going to write about wouldn't have happened if he hadn't gotten fired in the first place so it's kind of important to include that here.)

A. My family was shocked.

If you're telling a story, the best way to surprise the people who are reading it is to start off by saying how nice and sweet everything was, or what a lovely day it was, and then say that something horrible happened. Like, *It was a very beautiful day with sunshine when suddenly the whole town caught fire, and also my cat died.* That's much more alarming than saying *It was a dreary, gloomy day with a hint of mystery in the air when suddenly the whole town caught fire, and also my cat died.* Because the town catching fire and the dead cat kind of go along with dreariness and gloom. But with sunshine and a blue sky you're expecting something nice, like robins.

Anyway, before my father got fired, my family was happy and normal and good, like a sunshiny day. I'm talking about last spring now, since that's where the story starts—during the happy-normal-good time at the end of fourth grade. My family had had an exciting winter. My grandfather, Daddy Bo, had come to live with us for a few months while we looked for an old people's home for him to move to. By the way, every time I say "old people's home" Lexie rolls her eyes and corrects me. She says, "It's called a continuing care retirement community, Pearl" in this 14-year-old voice of hers. Whatever. The place we found is right here in New York City, so Daddy Bo is closer than ever. Plus, he really likes his apartment at The Towers.

My favorite part about when Daddy Bo was living with us was that I got to share Lexie's room since Daddy Bo was staying in mine. Unfortunately, I have to point out that Lexie wasn't too thrilled with the arrangement.

She likes her privacy, and she was used to doing all sorts of interesting teenage things—phoning her many, many best friends; applying makeup, etc., etc., etc.—behind her closed door. Now I had crept into her personal space. I found it fascinating, but Lexie was relieved to have her room back after Daddy Bo moved to The Towers.

Anyway, the day I have chosen as my story-starter is a Wednesday at the end of the month of May. Lexie had met JBIII and me at Emily Dickinson Elementary, and now she was walking us back to Twelfth Street. Her violin was slung over her shoulder, and she had so many books with her that she had brought her wheelie cart to school that morning. She said that if she didn't use it she might get a neck injury or become a hunchback.

JBIII tried to make conversation with my sister even though I could tell that this was one of those afternoons when Lexie's mind was tied up with something important, probably only to her.

"You sure do have a lot of books with you," JBIII commented. He actually seemed interested in what she might say back to him. We'd been trailing behind Lexie to avoid the wheelie cart, but now JBIII trotted along at her side.

"I have finals," said Lexie.

"Final whats?" JBIII wanted to know.

"Exams."

Lexie was not in a talkative mood, but JBIII didn't

seem to notice. He doesn't have any brothers or sisters, but that wasn't exactly the problem since frankly it's hard to know how an eighth-grade girl is going to react to anything. Just FYI, I want to go on record as saying that when I'm in eighth grade I will be completely predictable and pleasant.

JBIII was impressed. "Wow, you already have final exams? I thought only college students had to take those."

Lexie brightened. She'd been flicking away at her cell phone with her one free thumb, but now she clicked off the phone and turned her attention to JBIII. "Oh, no. We have finals in middle school. This is my second year taking finals. There is SO much studying involved."

"I can imagine," said JBIII, since studying is right up his alley.

I avoided something slimy in the street and then paused to look in the window of a bakery. I don't like sweet things, but it is amazing what you can do with frosting. I saw a cupcake with a snail on the top, which is disgusting even if you like snails, but still sort of fascinating, and a cake in the shape of a baby buggy and another cake that looked just like Bitey—if he had orange fur, which he doesn't, and green eyes, which he also doesn't.

I ran to catch up with JBIII and Lexie, and we turned onto our street. We walked by people who were sitting on their stoops, since it was such a nice day, but suddenly we had to hide in a doorway because we had spotted Mrs.

Mott from my apartment building. Mrs. Mott is about three hundred years old but she has a voice like a blaring tuba and she marches around New York as if she's the queen and we are all her serfs. She could learn a lot from the motto, "If you can't say something nice, don't say anything at all"—although then she would probably never have anything to say again for the rest of her life, which actually would be just fine with me.

"Is she gone yet?" I whispered from the doorway.

"Who are we hiding from again?" asked JBIII. He hadn't been my new best friend for very long and so he hadn't had any embarrassing encounters with Mrs. Mott yet.

"Mrs. Mott," Lexie told him.

"Who's Mrs. Mott?"

But before my sister could answer JBIII, Mrs. Mott took a break from charging down the street to poke her head in our doorway and say, "For pity's sake, what are you children doing in here? This isn't your building."

Well, duh.

I glanced at Lexie, who I thought was going to die from having been called a child, and I almost replied, "Hiding from you," but Lexie clapped her hand over my mouth, glared at Mrs. Mott, and said all haughty, "I am quite sure we know where we live, thank you." Then she hauled her wheelie out of the doorway and headed up Twelfth Street again.

Her cheeks were flaming.

JBIII and I hurried after her.

When we reached our building, JBIII's mother was waiting to walk him across the street to his own building.

"Bye!" JBIII and I called to each other. "See you tomorrow!" Then I ran after Lexie, who was striding furiously through the lobby. I don't think she had even greeted John. When she's really mad she can't speak to anyone except Valerie.

"Hi, John," I said, pausing at his desk. I didn't want him to think that both the Littlefield girls were rude, plus I really like him.

"Hello, Pearl. How was school?"

"Oh. You know." I don't usually like answering that question, but I don't mind too much when John asks it. "Only nineteen days left," I informed him. "Then vacation."

"And how many days of vacation?"

"Seventy-six." I had figured that out in February.

I caught up with Lexie at the elevator and we rode to the seventh floor. On the way I searched through my backpack for the key to our apartment. My very own key. I had only had it for a couple of weeks, and I was extremely proud of it. It had been my most important birthday present. I didn't have a computer or a cell phone, but now at last I had a key to our apartment. I had gotten it at my tenth birthday party, which we had already had the party even though my birthday wasn't until the beginning of summer vacation. That was why we'd had the party. Because if we'd waited until my actual birthday all my friends would have been at soccer camp or dude ranches.

I hustled past Lexie when we reached our floor and ran down the hall to our apartment, #7F, the key clutched in my hand. I opened the door slowly because sometimes Bitey likes to race out into the hallway and then he hisses when you pick him up to bring him home. But he wasn't in sight.

"We're home!" I called as Lexie stepped in behind me.

Mom stuck her head out of her office. My mother is a writer. She writes books for children. Her name is Adrienne Read Blackburn Littlefield, but on the covers of the books it just says A. Littlefield. I don't know why.

"How was school?" asked Mom.

"Oh. You know," I said. I went into the kitchen to look for a snack.

In the hallway behind me I could hear Lexie giving Mom a much longer answer to her question. Something about an A on a paper and an A on a test and an A on a quiz and also an A on a pop quiz.

"Plus," Lexie continued, "Dallas invited me to a movie on Saturday."

Dallas was Lexie's boyfriend. Lexie got all A's *and* she had a boyfriend.

Lexie headed for her room and closed her door. What a surprise.

Mom went back in her office and closed her door, too. She was working on a new book, something about a girl whose best friend moves away. This was interesting because my best friend, Justine, had moved away in January. She hadn't moved far—just to another neighborhood—so we still got to see each other sometimes. But Lexie thought that the move had been good for me. Justine was only in first grade and Lexie felt I should branch out and find a friend who was my own age, which is how I had gotten JBIII as my new best friend. (But Justine was still my old best friend.) I wondered if the girls in Mom's book were a first grader and a fourth grader like Justine and me, and then I wondered how I felt about that. I decided it would be okay as long as the characters weren't named Justine and Pearl. And maybe it would be a good idea if they didn't live in New York City, either.

We only had a little homework that day, and I did it in a hurry, sitting at the desk in my room and repeatedly sliding Bitey off of the worksheets I was filling in. Then I got bored for a while, but then, after only half an hour of boredness, our front door opened and in walked my father and Daddy Bo.

"Hi, Daddy Bo!" I cried, running to him. I threw my arms around his waist. I didn't bother to throw my arms around my father since I had just seen him that morning.

"Pearl!" said Daddy Bo. "My gem of a granddaughter."

Lexie came out of her room then, not running, but still everyone could tell that she was happy to see Daddy Bo, too.

We all sat in the family room for a while and talked. Nobody had to do anything about dinner since Dad and Daddy Bo had picked up take-out food at Hong Fu, which is Chinese food, which I love, except for the tiny red things that you have to watch out for because some of them make your eyes water.

"So," said Daddy Bo as I leaned into his side. He and I were sitting on the couch, along with Bitey. Mom and Dad and Lexie were sitting in chairs. "Tell me about your summer vacation plans."

Now that's the kind of question I like to answer. "Camp first," I told him. "For the month of July."

"Camp Merrimac again?"

"Yup." Camp Merrimac is a day camp that Lexie and I have gone to for lots of summers. It's in New Jersey—not the part that smells bad and has smokestacks, but the part where there are fir trees and lakes and owls—so we take a bus there every day. It's an arts camp. You have to pay attention to the word "arts" because in this case, "arts" doesn't just mean painting desert islands and folding up origami cranes; it means other kinds of art as well, which I guess is why the camp brochure says "arts" not "art." Like for instance, music is an art and so is dancing and so is acting. So Camp Merrimac is perfect for both Lexie and me because my big sister can concentrate on her music and I can do arts and crafts. Plus there are regular camp activities, like swimming and going on field trips and tromping around in the woods with your bug journal.

"And is Justine going to camp with you?" asked Daddy Bo.

I nodded. "It will be her second year. Guess who else is going—JBThree. His first time."

"You're going to have quite a summer," commented Daddy Bo. "Camp in July and your big trip in August."

I was impressed that Daddy Bo had such a good grasp on our plans because, not to be mean, but sometimes he's a little bit forgetful.

My father cleared his throat then. "Speaking of our trip," he said, "your mom and I have a surprise for you girls."

I couldn't imagine how our trip could get any better. My family and I were going to visit the Wild West. We were going to fly out to Wyoming and see ghost towns and geysers. Then we were going to take a train to Arizona and ride donkeys in the Grand Canyon. We were going to see redwood forests and stay in giant hotels in national parks. I planned to buy a cowboy hat.

"What is it?" I cried, leaping to my feet. "What's the surprise?"

Mom and Dad smiled at each other, and Daddy Bo said, "I'm going with you."

Now I began jumping up and down like Justine used to do when she was excited. "Really?" I exclaimed 4x, because I just couldn't believe it.

Lexie was grinning. "Excellent!" she said.

"But Daddy Bo, are you allowed to ride horses?" I asked suddenly. I hoped I didn't sound rude, but, well, Daddy Bo is on the rickety side, and in the fall he had had an accident and broken his shoulder.

"No," admitted Daddy Bo. "I can't go hiking, either. But that's okay. I'll still be able to do plenty of things. Can you believe I've never seen the Grand Canyon?"

We all started talking about what we hoped to do on our fabulous trip to the Wild West. Mom set the food from Hong Fu on the table, and we ate sweet and sour chicken and moo goo gai pan, which I'm still not sure what it was even after eating it, and vegetable chow mein. And everyone except me ate hot and spicy shrimp with garlic sauce. And all the time we talked about the Wild West and what a great summer it was going to be.

So this is the part of the story that's like the sunshiny day. Now get ready for the alarming part.

I. My dad got fired.

    A. My family was shocked.

Since I've already mentioned that something alarming is about to happen, and let's face it, since you know what that alarming thing is because it's right there in my outline for Ms. Brody, I'll just cut to the chase (as my mom would say).

Our happiness about Daddy Bo and the trip to the Wild West lasted exactly one week. It ended the next Wednesday when Dad came home from work. He came home an hour earlier than usual, which should have been a clue that something was wrong, because one thing about my father is that he likes sticking to a routine. But it was his last day of work before summer vacation, so I thought maybe he just wanted to get an extra hour of relaxation in.

Here's why my dad gets a summer vacation: He's a teacher. Well, actually he's a professor. Well, actually he *was* a professor. I'm not sure what he is now that he's been fired. But for my whole life up until the first week of June this year, he taught economics at a college in NYC. Frankly, I'm not sure why anyone would want to take economics, let alone teach it. If you look through a college catalogue it's one of the most boring classes listed. Don't sign up for it unless you really want to know all about the production of goods and services and how this production affects business and finance. But apparently a lot of students did want to know about those things, and they signed up to take my dad's class, and he was one of the most popular professors at the college.

I guess he wasn't popular enough, though. Or else maybe everyone finally figured out how boring economics is and they stopped signing up for the class even though my father was teaching it. At any rate, on that Wednesday when Dad came home early, instead of looking happy about the beginning of his summer vacation, which I'd like to point out was almost three weeks before the beginning of *my* summer vacation, he looked stunned, and not in a good way. He looked like I probably did last Christmas when Justine told me she was moving to a different part of the city and we wouldn't be going to the same school anymore.

"What's the matter, Dad?" I asked as he sat down on the couch and put his head in his hands.

I was doing my homework in the living room because Lexie was practicing the violin in her bedroom, and sometimes it's better to be far away from all the screeching and plucking.

But Dad didn't answer my question. He just said, "Is your mother in her office?"

I was going to give him a smart answer since where else would Mom be, but his expression was scaring me. "Yes," I said.

Dad disappeared into Mom's office and closed the door behind him. He didn't come out for a very long time, and when he did he looked grim, like he'd looked when Daddy Bo was in the hospital. Then Mom came out of the office and her eyes were all red.

"Pearl, please go get your sister," said my father.

I knocked on Lexie's door, and even though Dad hadn't told me to say this, I called, "Family meeting!"

"What, right now?" said Lexie. "Dad isn't even home."

"Yes, he is. And he wants us in the living room."

We gathered in about two seconds.

"Everything all right?" Lexie asked my mother, looking at her red eyes. She was probably wondering if Mom was having trouble with her characters again. Sometimes they misbehave (according to Mom) and then my mother gets crabby and it's a good idea not to bother her with questions about my allowance or whether she'll let me go to a movie with a PG-13 rating.

Mom nodded but didn't say anything, so Lexie turned to Dad. "You called a family meeting?" She flopped next to me on the couch.

"Not exactly," replied Dad. "Pearl said we were having a family meeting. I just need to talk to everyone." He removed his glasses and polished them on his shirt. With his glasses off I thought he looked like a little boy. He blinked at us and put the glasses on and then he was himself again. But not really, since something was wrong.

Bitey jumped into my lap and for once let me hold him and pat him without swatting at my hand.

"Well," said my father. He'd been sitting down, but now he stood up. "I have some bad news."

"Is it Daddy Bo?" cried Lexie. "Did something happen to Daddy Bo?"

"No, no," said Dad. "It's—well, I was fired today." He looked around at Mom and Lexie and me, and then he sat on the arm of my mother's chair and rubbed her shoulder sadly.

"Oh, no," said my sister, and her hand flew to her mouth.

"What does this mean?" I asked.

"It means Dad doesn't have a job anymore," snapped Lexie.

"I know what 'fired' means," I replied. "Duh. But what does it *mean*?" I was pretty sure that Dad had been fired because everyone had realized how boring economics is. But maybe there was another college where the students hadn't caught onto the boringness yet and Dad could teach economics there. Or maybe he could teach something else at his old college. On the other hand, if Dad wasn't working maybe he would have more free time. Even on his so-called summer vacation he was always preparing lectures and writing articles, but now, well, suddenly I had very nice visions of playing game after game of Boggle with my father and going to PG-13 movies with him and riding our bikes in the park. This was why I wanted to know what being fired meant for our future, but I had forgotten that when Lexie is nervous she covers up by turning into an old-timey schoolmarm.

I stood up, faced Lexie, and curtsied. "Excuse me, ma'am. What I meant to say was, 'Father, what are the *implications* of the firing incident?'"

I didn't get an answer to my question, though, and I was kind of relieved, because even I knew I was being smart (okay, rude). No one was paying attention to me. This was because my mother had put her arms around my father and (get ready for something really scary) my father had started to cry a little. He didn't wail the way

Justine used to do, but his eyes got watery and he couldn't speak.

My mom led Dad out of the family room and back into her office.

"Wait!" cried Lexie, and now she jumped to her feet. "What does this mean?" she called after them.

I sat on the couch with Bitey in my lap. He was sound asleep. "It means he doesn't have a job anymore," I told my sister.

Lexie scowled at me, went to her room, and closed the door. At least she didn't slam it.

No one felt like eating dinner that night, including me, even though we were having leftovers, which is my favorite kind of meal because it's the one time I can eat moo goo gai pan, Count Chocula, and olives without Lexie telling me I'm disgusting. I stared at my fake chocolate cereal and everyone else stared at their food and finally Lexie said, "Dad? Why did you get fired?"

"Cutbacks," Dad answered. "The economy is in trouble, you know."

I wondered why, as an economics professor, Dad hadn't seen this coming, but I didn't say anything.

"You mean the college couldn't afford you?" asked Lexie.

Dad nodded. "Six professors, two librarians, and several members of the office staff were let go along with me. Other people were asked to take pay cuts. The college is hoping to have a balanced budget by the time school starts again in the fall."

"But who's going to teach your classes?" I wanted to know.

"There are two other economics professors," said Dad, "and my students will be divided between them. They'll be teaching much larger classes for a lot less money."

"Why—?" I started to say.

But Mom interrupted me. "Maybe we should have another meeting after dinner."

I didn't see why we couldn't have one now, since we were all together, but whatever.

As soon as dinner was over Mom and Dad and Lexie and Bitey and I sat down in the family room again. Ordinarily, Lexie and I don't like family meetings, since our parents usually call them so that they can discuss our behavior or attitudes or give us bad news. This time I wasn't nervous, though. It wasn't going to be a pleasant meeting, but at least I knew I wasn't in trouble for anything.

"I'm sure you girls have plenty of questions," said Mom, starting the meeting.

Lexie nodded solemnly. "What I've been wondering," she said, "is whether we'll have enough money without Dad's salary."

That's funny. What I was going to ask was if Dad and I could have a Boggle tournament in all his spare time.

Mom and Dad looked at each other, which was not a good sign. It meant they were trying to figure out how to give Lexie and me more bad news. Finally Dad said, "We'll be all right without my salary for a while, but we *will* have to cut back."

I hoped that Lexie's violin lessons would be the first thing to go.

"You mean like not eat out in restaurants so often?" asked Lexie.

"Actually," said my mother, "for a while, we won't be eating in restaurants at all. Well, except for very special occasions, like Pearl's birthday. And no more take-out food and pizzas. It's expensive, and it all adds up. Cooking and eating at home is cheaper."

"There are lots of small ways we can cut back," added my father. "We'll have Family Game Nights instead of going to the movies. Or we'll rent DVDs. We'll buy cheaper brands at the supermarket. I think that if we pay attention to what we spend our money on, we'll find plenty of ways to save and be thrifty."

Dad should know.

Mom rolled her neck around then, like she had a headache, which she probably did. She gazed past Lexie and me, out into the hallway, and finally she said, "Also, there's one big thing we can do right away that will save quite a bit of money." Now she focused on my sister and me, looking at us over her glasses. "We're going to have to cancel the trip with Daddy Bo."

"Our trip to the Wild West?" I cried. I said this so loudly that Bitey's tail puffed up like a blowfish and he ran out of the room. "No! Please. We aren't going anywhere else this summer and everyone in my class is going to a dude ranch or soccer camp or the beach. We have to go *some*where."

"I'm sorry," said Mom. "The trip is very expensive, and we haven't paid for most of it yet."

My sister turned to me then and said, "Do you have any idea how much rent is, Pearl?"

"Do you have any idea how annoying you are, Lexie?"

"Pearl," said my father.

"Sorry, Lexie."

"What about Camp Merrimac?" asked Lexie, without bothering to say, *That's okay, Pearl.*

"Camp is already paid for," Dad replied, "so you can still go."

I crossed my arms. When I had said I wanted to go somewhere this summer, I had not meant New Jersey.

"Maybe you could get your money back from Camp Merrimac," said Lexie, although she didn't really look like she meant it.

Mom shook her head. "We paid for it last fall. It's non-refundable."

Lexie glanced at me. "'Non-refundable' means they won't give us our money back."

"Duh," I said. Then I added, "'Duh' means that you should stop talking now."

"Girls!" exclaimed Dad. "Enough. The last thing we need is bickering. Please focus."

So we talked for a little while about how Mom would still be earning money with her writing, and then Lexie suggested that we could clean our own apartment instead of paying Mrs. Yardley to do it, but Dad pointed out that we didn't want to take Mrs. Yardley's job away from her so we would wait and see, and I said that maybe we could all cut each other's hair.

We were beginning to feel tired then, so my mother said, "Meeting adjourned," and we went to our bedrooms. I stared at my homework papers and decided not to study for our spelling quiz. I wandered back to the family room and phoned JBIII. "My dad got fired," I told him, and JBIII said he didn't know anyone who had ever been fired. "How does it feel when your father gets fired?" he asked, and I replied, "Not good."

Back in my bedroom I sat at my desk and took out a pad of paper. Across the top I wrote Pearl's Income and Expenses, which seemed like the right way to consider a matter of economics. On the left side of the paper I wrote Income, and under that I wrote:

Allowance

Birthday money???

That was it. I had no other sources of income. Lexie sometimes babysat (the most embarrassing times were when she babysat for me) or tutored little kids who were having trouble with math, but no one paid me to do anything yet.

I moved to the other side of the paper and wrote Expenses. Underneath that I wrote:

Savings (I was supposed to put 1/3 of my allowance in the bank)

Donations (I was supposed to donate 1/3 of my allowance to good causes, such as firefighters and sick cats)

Art supplies

Additional parts to my pirate costume

Movies that Mom and Dad think are not worth their own $$

I tried to figure out how much my expenses might total this summer, and after doing a very long addition problem I realized they were much higher than my income, even if Daddy Bo gave me quite a bit of $$ on my birthday.

Okay. Well, there were ways to cut, which should make Mom and Dad proud. I looked at the Expenses side of the paper again and drew a line through Savings and then through Donations. There. That was better. Then I decided that I could wait until Halloween to add any parts to my pirate costume, so I crossed out that line.

And I had a feeling nobody in my family was going to be going to the movies this summer, so I crossed out the last line too. I was left with Art Supplies. That seemed reasonable. I could tell my parents they could cut my allowance in half. But then I remembered a few other things I'd been meaning to buy, so I added some items to my expenses: iPod, more stuffed animals, hamster (alive, not stuffed), hamster environment, cowboy hat, geode, snow globe of Old Faithful geyser. I'd been planning to get the last three items on our trip to the Wild West, and I still wanted them.

I totaled up my new expenses and realized I would need a raise in my allowance, but it didn't seem like the right time to ask for one, so finally I stuffed the papers in my desk and went to bed.

I. My dad got fired.

    A. My family was shocked.

    B. We tried to pretend that saving $$ was fun!!!

The next morning as Dad and Lexie and I rode downstairs in the elevator, Dad said, "Lexie, I can pick up Pearl and JB this afternoon."

I thought about saying, "Dad, it's JB*Three*," but I didn't know if it was nice to correct a fired person.

"That's okay. I can do it," said Lexie.

"No, really. I'm free."

"Well, anyway, it's only me," I spoke up. "JBThree has to go to the dentist this afternoon. He might need braces. He's not walking *to* school with us either, because he's going out for breakfast with his parents." Dad looked a little sad when I said that, so I stopped talking.

The elevator doors slid open then, and we all said hi to Mr. Thompson who was sitting on a bench with his dog, Hammer. Mr. Thompson and Hammer are both very old and creaky and have to rest a lot.

Lexie saw Valerie waiting for her outside and picked up her pace. "Bye!" she called over her shoulder as she sped through the lobby. "Thanks for picking up Pearl, Dad." She raced through the door, saying "Valerie, you'll never guess what happened." I wondered how many of her friends my sister would spread the sad news to that day, but as Lexie and Valerie walked away, I heard Lexie say, "Dallas never called me last night, and I left him *seven* messages." Huh. The bad news was about Dallas.

"So what are you going to do today, Dad?" I asked as we started down Twelfth Street. The sky was perfectly blue, probably just like the sky you would see on a nice morning in the Wild West.

I was a little bit jealous of my father, since he didn't have to go to work.

My father clapped his hands together. "I'm going to start looking for a new job," he said smartly. He said this in the cheerful tone adults use when they're talking to kids about things that aren't fun at all but that they're trying to make *sound* fun. Like, "I'll bet we can clean out your whole closet in half an hour! Wouldn't it be great if we found your bubble blaster in there?" (The bubble blaster was something I had lost after just one day, and my parents said if I wanted another I would have to spend my own $$ on it.)

I glanced at my father. "You're already going to start looking for a job?"

"Absolutely."

"You aren't going to take off even one day?"

"Finding another job won't be easy."

"But could we do something fun after school?"

"We'll see. I told your mom we'd run errands after I pick you up."

"What errands do we have to do?" I asked. I hoped we weren't going to the dry cleaner, which smells a little bit like gasoline and also a little bit like Bitey's breath.

We passed the deli and I waved to Mrs. Chin, who works at the bagel counter. She smiled and waved back, mouthing "Hi, Pearl!" through the window.

"Grocery store," said Dad, "stationery store, shoe store—"

"Who needs shoes?" I wanted to know.

"Nobody. I just need shoelaces."

I'm sorry to admit it, but the errands didn't sound like a whole lot of fun. I thought things over during spelling class, though, and decided to be cheerful for the sake of my father, the fired person.

I think he appreciated it. At the grocery store that

afternoon he put on his fake excited voice again and said, "I have an idea, Pearl. Let's make a game out of our shopping. We're only going to buy the least expensive brands, but I have a calculator in my pocket and I'll keep track of the prices of the brands we *would* have bought, so that after we check out we can compare the total on the calculator to the total on the cash register and see how much money we've saved!"

It actually did sound like fun, and when Dad read off the first item on the list—tissues—I ran right by all the boxes with cherry blossoms and leaping fish and sunsets on them and picked out one that was solid white except for the word BASICS written across the top in big black letters. I compared prices, and the BASICS tissues were definitely the cheapest.

"Excellent," said Dad.

I put four boxes of white BASICS tissues in our cart, and my father pulled out his calculator and clicked in the price of the brand we used to buy and multiplied it by four.

"Now what?" I asked.

"Seltzer," said Dad.

Guess what. There was BASICS seltzer, too, and also BASICS laundry detergent and dishwashing soap and quite a few other things, except not bananas or celery, but that was okay.

By the time we were checking out I was excited and

felt a little like jumping up and down. "You know what?" I said to Dad. "This would be a good experiment anyway, but it's even better since you got fired and we can really use the extra money."

A woman in the next line turned around and looked at us, and Dad said, "Remember when we talked about keeping certain things to yourself, Pearl?"

"Yup," I said, hopping from one foot to the other. I could not wait until the cashier had rung us up. When he had, I looked at the amount on the register while Dad looked at his calculator.

"Thirty-eight seventy-four," I announced. "What does the calculator say?"

"Fifty-one sixty-two. And that's without the tax."

"Yes!" I cried. "We saved almost fifteen dollars." (It was amazing how fast I could do math in my head when it was for something really important, instead of for figuring out how many passengers would still be on a bus after a lot of people had gotten on and off, which is the opposite of important.) I smiled broadly at the woman in the other line.

The rest of our errands weren't quite as much fun as the grocery store, but it was nice to walk around our neighborhood with my father, especially since we weren't in a rush. We watched some pigeons fight over a bran muffin, and then I entered a contest in a bookstore. I didn't really want the prize, which was a coupon for

$100 worth of kids' books, but I thought that if I won I could give the coupon to Mr. Potter, my teacher. He could put the books in our classroom. Plus, he would feel guilty the next time he had to keep me inside during recess to finish my undone homework.

After I had entered the contest, Dad and I tried to guess the names of all the dogs we saw people walking.

Finally Dad said we ought to be getting home. "I'm going to cook dinner tonight," he told me.

"I'll help."

And I did. So all in all, my father's first day as a fired person was a lot of fun.

After that, the fun part faded quickly.

The next night, Friday, we were all tired from school and work and job hunting. It was just the kind of night when ordering pizza would have put us in a better mood. But when I suggested it, Mom said, "Remember our new rules, Pearl."

I did not remember that we had actual rules. I remembered that we were supposed to cut down on our spending. So I said, "Dad and I saved fifteen dollars at the grocery store yesterday. Let's use that money."

"But then we won't have saved it," Lexie pointed out, looking at me with a sad frown, the same look she might have given to a lost dog that was limping down the street.

"I know!" said Mom. "We have a pizza from the grocery store in the freezer. We'll just heat that up."

"Is that the pizza with the really flat crust, the tiny slices, and all the vegetables?" I asked. We keep grocery-store pizza in the freezer in case there's an emergency, like a blackout or a blizzard, and there's no food in any of the stores or restaurants in all of Manhattan and we have to eat up the stuff in our kitchen just to stay alive.

My mother sighed. "I don't know, Pearl. It's pizza. You wanted pizza, and we have pizza. So let's eat it."

That was my clue not to make any more mean comments about the freezer food.

It was about four days later when I noticed how messy our family room had become. This was because now it was not only our family room, living room, and dining room but Dad's new office, too. In addition to looking for a job, he was writing articles and preparing talks, so he needed an office. I hadn't realized how much stuff he'd had in his real office at the college until he brought it all home with him. By the next week his computer was sitting on our dining table. A lot of little boxes with knobs and buttons and flashing lights were connected to the computer with a big tangle of cords that Bitey liked to nap on. Also on the table were piles of papers and a stack of files. And for some reason the fax machine from my mother's office had been moved into the family room and was also sitting on the table, which I think you couldn't call it a table anymore. It was Dad's desk. From then on when we ate meals we could either eat at the desk with Dad shouting, "Don't spill on the keyboard!" every ten seconds, or on the couch with Mom shouting, "Don't spill on the cushions!" every ten seconds. It was not a relaxing dining atmosphere, but what with the freezer pizza and the BASICS food I didn't really care.

"I have an idea," I said on Tuesday night after I had finished a bowl of spaghetti. (I had eaten it sitting cross-legged on the floor on an old, holey sheet in case I spilled.)

"Yes?" said Dad.

"How about if you set up your office in my bedroom and I move in with Lexie again?"

Lexie, who was eating gingerly on the couch, set her own bowl of spaghetti on the coffee table and shot to her feet. "Absolutely not! No!"

"But we had so much fun. And anyway, I would like to make that sacrifice for Dad. Wouldn't you like to help out, too?" I asked my enraged sister.

Lexie swiveled toward my parents, who were eating by the computer and fax machine. "Do I have—?" she started to say.

"That's a very nice offer, Pearl," Mom spoke up, "but

you may keep your room. This is only a temporary situation."

Lexie sat down again. "Thank you."

One Saturday, when Dad had been a fired person for ten days, my parents said that we needed to go grocery shopping again but not at our usual store.

"We're going to Brooklyn," announced Dad.

"Brooklyn!" I exclaimed.

"It isn't *that* far away, Pearl," said Lexie.

"It feels far away. Why are we going to Brooklyn?"

"Because there's a BuyMore-PayLess on Third Avenue," Mom replied, "and it has the cheapest prices of any store around. We'll get our groceries there."

"We've made up a big shopping list so we won't have to go back for a while," added Dad.

"And," said Mom, "what do you think—we're going to take the subway!"

"But a cab—"

"No cabs, Pearl. Too expensive," said Dad.

I imagined my family struggling onto a crowded subway car, trying to hold on to the poles and our bags of groceries at the same time. Of the four of us, I was the most likely to lose my balance, drop the groceries, and fall down.

"Do I have to go?" asked Lexie suddenly from the

doorway of her bedroom. I thought maybe her eyes looked a little red. And watery.

Mom must have thought so, too, because she only hesitated for a second before she said, "No, honey. You can stay at home. Everything all right?"

"Yup," replied Lexie. And then she closed her door quietly.

"Has anyone noticed that Dallas hasn't come over lately?" I asked.

Mom and Dad both gave me a Look so I didn't make any more comments about the missing boyfriend.

The subway trip to Brooklyn was fun. One time the brakes slammed on when we weren't expecting it and a man toppled over and landed on his bottom and said a word I'm not allowed to say, and then also a lost pigeon hopped into our car and wandered around cooing. These kinds of things almost never happen in a cab.

We bought six overflowing bags of groceries and supplies at BuyMore-PayLess, and then we struggled back to the subway station with them. The ride home was not fun at all. Nothing interesting happened, and it was hard to keep track of our bags, which were really heavy, and there were no empty seats, but at least I didn't fall down.

When we finally made it home I said, "The next time we go to BuyMore-PayLess why don't we take our car?"

We had a green Subaru that we parked in the garage in the basement of our apartment building.

Dad set the last bag of groceries on the kitchen counter and let out a sigh. He glanced at Mom. "I'm afraid we've decided to sell the car," he said.

"What! *Why?*" (I liked our car.)

"Partly because it's in good condition and we can get a couple of thousand dollars for it, but mostly because keeping it in the garage is expensive. Our garage bill is huge. Without the car we can save hundreds of dollars every month."

"But—but—" There was a gumball machine in the garage that I really liked, in addition to our Subaru.

"I'm sorry, Pearl," said Mom, "but we have to make some difficult choices."

"I'm earning a little money writing articles for journals," added Dad, "but not nearly as much as I was earning when I was teaching. And I can tell that the job hunt is going to take a long time. A lot of other people are out of work, too, and we're all competing for the same jobs."

I figured that the least I could do was not have a fit in front of my parents. Dad already felt bad, plus he was working awfully hard in his new office in our family room. So I went into my room before I began to cry. Then I threw my hairbrush on the floor and it broke, and I had to hide it in the back of my closet.

It was during supper that night that Dad said, "Family meeting in ten minutes."

"Oh, no!" I cried. "*Now* what happened?"

But it turned out that the meeting was for a nice reason. When Lexie and I were seated on the couch, Mom and Dad came into the family room with their hands behind their backs. With a flourish Mom handed me a large blue album and Dad handed Lexie a large purple album.

"They're scrapbooks," said Mom. "Maybe we aren't taking our trip out west, but you girls are still going to Camp Merrimac, and I have a feeling that other fun things will happen this summer."

"So we thought you might like to keep a record of them by making scrapbooks," said Dad.

I flipped through the blank album, imagining the possibilities.

"You can glue postcards and photos to the pages," said Mom.

"Or make drawings," added Dad, looking at me. "Or write diary entries."

"And we can decorate the pages!" I exclaimed, thinking of my supply of papers and markers and stickers and sequins.

I glanced at Lexie. She isn't very arty, but even she looked intrigued.

I jumped to my feet. "Thank you," I said, and kissed Mom and Dad. Then I hurried to my room, closed my door, and sat at my desk, the scrapbook opened to the first page. In my very best handwriting I wrote:

Today we took subway to Brooklyn for a grocery shopping experience. A man fell down and swore, and a pigeon rode with us for two stops, exciting!

I illustrated the page with a drawing of a bag of groceries, a drawing of a man crashing to the floor and saying !#%!* in a cartoon bubble, and a drawing of a pigeon holding a swipe card for the subway under his wing.

I. My dad got fired.

  A. My family was shocked.

  B. We tried to pretend that saving $$ was fun!!!

  C. We had a tiny celebration when I hit the big one-oh.

Since I am the youngest person in my family, everyone else has already hit the big one-oh and progressed from lame nine, which only has one number in it, to ten, double digits. Even Bitey has turned ten, although when he turned ten it was in cat years, so he actually turned from sixty-three to seventy. He skipped the big one-oh entirely. Although come to think of it, he was the first one of us to hit the big seven-oh. Anyway, since there was no one else left in our entire family who would turn ten after I did, I thought Mom and Dad and Lexie would make a big deal out of my one-oh. Plus, I kind of felt I deserved it, what with all the cutting back we'd been doing, and the fact that my trip to the Wild West had been cancelled and I might never get to see a ghost town or a redwood or a pack mule. I decided not to say much about my birthday, though. I figured that was how a mature 10-year-old would handle the situation.

A week before my birthday came one of the best days of the entire year—the last day of school. Bitey woke me up early that morning by staring at me. I opened my eyes and saw his round yellow cat eyes just inches away. I pulled my head back.

"Hi, Bitey," I said. He was probably hungry. I sat up, yawned, and pulled off my nightgown. There was a rip in the side so big, I could fit my whole head through it.

"Why don't you learn to sew?" Lexie had asked when she'd seen the rip.

There were about ten zillion mean things I could have said to Lexie right then, but I had settled on a non-mean reply, which was, "I like the rip."

I put on my last-day-of-school clothes, which I had chosen the night before and laid out on a chair. It took me about six seconds to get dressed. This was one of the few things that I did far, far better than Lexie, who practically had a stroke every morning trying to choose an appropriate outfit for a day of eighth grade.

Bitey stared at me from the doorway while I got

dressed, then from the hallway while I was in the bath-room, and then from the kitchen while I walked through our apartment. In the cupboard I found a can of his new food, which I don't think he likes it very much. He doesn't appreciate change.

"Why can't he have his old food?" I'd asked Mom the first time I'd found the dull-looking green cans on Bitey's shelf. They said simply ORGANIC CAT FOOD on them. No pictures of kitties wearing crowns or eating with silver-ware that someone had glued onto fake white cat paws.

"Because this is the same as his old food," Mom had replied, "but it only costs half as much."

"Are you sure it's the same?" I'd said as I'd watched Bitey sniff it and jump away from his dish as if the food had shouted at him.

"Positive. I compared the ingredients. Exactly the same."

Huh.

When I spooned the food into Bitey's dish on the last day of school he ate it all, which was my clue that it was going to be a very, very good day.

And it was.

In school, Mr. Potter let us sit wherever we wanted, so JBIII and I waited until Jill-Rachel-Katie had chosen seats (they sat in their *own* seats, the ones they had already sat in all year, which only goes to show you how unimagina-tive they are), and then my best friend and I sat together by the windows, where we could look into the apartment building across the street, and also where we were about as far from Jill-Rachel-Katie as we could get.

All day long we only did things like clean out our desks and have a spelling bee and take turns talking about what we were going to do over vacation. When it was my turn I walked to the front of the classroom and said, "After I get day camp out of the way at the beginning of the summer, my family and I are going to travel to the Wild West. We're going to ride mules down into the Grand Canyon and see a redwood forest and spend the night in a ghost town." (As long as I was lying, I might as well be creative.) "Oh, and we're going to pan for gold and sleep under the stars on a dude ranch and look for stallions with some cowboys." I noticed a funny look on Mr. Potter's face then and figured he knew I was lying, so I decided to stop talking. "Thank you," I finished up. "I'll be sure to send po—" I was about to say "postcards" when I realized that of course I couldn't send anyone postcards from the west if I wasn't actually going there. "Um, have a happy summer," I said, and hurried to my seat.

I sat down heavily, then turned to look at JBIII, who was staring at me with his mouth open. I sent him a signal with my eyes that said, "SHH," and he didn't say anything, so I knew my signal was a good one.

Even though we didn't have to do any work, the day

seemed endless, like the time my father took me to the Museum of Modern Art and dragged me around from one painting to another until finally we got to the gift shop, where I bought a twisty straw for slurping up the milk from my Count Chocula.

I squirmed in my seat. I watched the hands on the clock, which I finally decided the clock might be broken. I was staring at Jill and remembering the time she had barfed on her desk when at last the buzzer sounded and Mr. Potter said, "Make sure you have all your belongings, people. Enjoy your vacations!"

I shot up out of my seat, took one last look at the corner of the blackboard where my name had been written every time I hadn't turned in my homework, called, "Bye, Mr. Potter!" and ran into the hall. For one second I felt bad for Mr. Potter and all teachers, since what their students really want is to get away from them. Then, clutching an armful of old paintings and tests and reports (I had forgotten my backpack), I charged through the hallway with JBIII at my heels.

We burst onto the street and found my father waiting for us, my backpack in his hands. I stuffed the papers into it, and Dad said, "Last day of school. I think this deserves a celebration." He took us to the Daily Grind, where JBIII said, "I have my own money, sir," and reached into his pocket.

I had zero money but Dad must have been thinking

about the hundreds of $$$ we were saving every month by not having our green Subaru anymore, because he bought me a tall lemonade, plus one for himself. After that I saw Lexie and three of her friends peer through the window and catch sight of us with our drinks and then hurry away, probably to Cuppa Joe, where it would be easier for Lexie to pretend she was a grown-up if Dad and JBIII and I weren't nearby.

After school I lay on the couch in the family room and was allowed to watch cartoons until dinnertime. It was a little hard to hear them over Dad's computer and fax machine and the ringing of his cell phone, but I managed. It was the perfect way to start summer vacation.

A week later came my big one-oh.

Now, it is true that I had already had a birthday party for my big one-oh. I'd had a party with my friends in the spring when everyone was still around. It's pointless to have a birthday party over summer vacation because no one can ever come to it. I didn't know what kind of family party to expect now that I had a fired person for a father, but I was hoping we could splurge since I was the last Littlefield to turn ten.

When Lexie turned thirteen we'd gone to the Hard Rock Café for her family party. Mom and Dad had had to make a reservation, and they'd ordered a cake ahead of time, and when the waiters had brought it to our table they'd sung to Lexie, which she only pretended to be embarrassed, because you could tell she hoped everyone in the restaurant was looking at her and feeling amazed that there was another teenager in the world.

"Happy birthday!" Mom and Dad said to me at breakfast on my actual one-oh. Lexie didn't join in because she was still snoring away in her bedroom. When I am a teenager I plan to be awake as much as possible so as not to miss anything.

"Thank you," I replied. I looked at Bitey then and he hissed at me, so after breakfast I made a sign for him that I taped to the bottom of the refrigerator where he could see it. It said:

All day I wondered about my special birthday dinner. I knew Daddy Bo would come with us, and I thought maybe we would go back to the Hard Rock Café, even though the Hard Rock Café isn't exactly my grandfather's kind of place, since it's crowded and noisy and Mom is always afraid that someone will knock into Daddy Bo and he'll fall over. Plus, in crowds Daddy Bo can't hear anything even with his hearing aids in, so then he takes the hearing aids out and one time he dropped one in some guacamole and my father cried, "Those cost eight hundred dollars each!"

Here are the nice things that happened on my big one-oh:

1. I got four birthday cards in the mail.

2. Bitey didn't hiss at me again.

3. Lexie took me to the Daily Grind and bought a lemonade for me and a Mocha Moxie for herself and we sat at a tiny round table just the two of us and suddenly I could see the point of being in public with no adults to tell you what to do.

At five thirty that afternoon I came out of my bedroom wearing a dress. I'd had to search a little while to find a dress in my closet, since I almost never wear them, and when I did find one it was on the tight side, but I wanted to look fancy for my special evening.

"Oh, my!" said Mom when I walked into the family room wearing my third-grade Christmas dress, which was velvet.

Lexie was sitting on the couch in her black jeans and

a tie-dyed T-shirt. I said to her, "Why aren't you dressed up?" and at the very same moment she said, "Pearl, you're going to swelter in that."

(Note: Look up "swelter" in the dictionary.)

"We don't have to get dressed up to go to Ollie's," Lexie replied.

Since Ollie's is just the diner on the corner this was my clue that my family had actually planned a surprise one-oh dinner for me at someplace very fancy, and Ollie's was a joke to throw me off the track. My parents must have decided that we could splurge. We were probably even going to take a cab.

I was a little surprised when we walked out of the apartment later and Lexie was still wearing her jeans and T-shirt and my parents were wearing jeans, too. Daddy Bo had arrived by then and he was wearing a suit, but then he almost always wears suits. We walked to the end of the block. I looked at Ollie's, then looked at my family, grinned, and hailed a cab.

"Pearl!" cried my father as the cab swerved over to the sidewalk. He stuck his head through the front window of the taxi and said to the driver, "Sorry, it was a mistake."

The cabdriver said the second bad word I'd heard recently, punched a button that swooped the window up so fast that it nearly hit my father on the chin, and then screeched back into the traffic on Sixth Avenue and I think he ran a red light.

"What are you *doing?*" cried Lexie, whose face had turned bright pink with embarrassment even though she didn't know the cabdriver or any of the people on the street.

"I—" I started to say, but then I saw my mother open the door to Ollie's. "Nothing," I muttered.

Well, by now you've probably figured out that my birthday dinner really was going to be at Ollie's and not at the Hard Rock Café or any other restaurant where I wouldn't look too out of place in a red velvet Christmas dress. We ate hamburgers and fries and drank Coke and no one came to our table with a cake, and even worse, the waitress said to me, "Don't you look pretty," which I know very well was really her way of saying, "What a strange clothing choice for a diner on a ninety-degree day, little girl."

At the end of the meal, the waitress brought the check and Daddy Bo reached for it, and my father let him pay for our food.

Back at the apartment Mom said, "Pearl, we have a surprise for you," but it was just that JBIII and his parents were coming over for the cake Mom had secretly baked while Lexie and I had been at the Daily Grind. And since I don't like cake anyway, I didn't even have a slice after everyone had finished singing "Happy Birth-day." I liked JBIII's present, which was a book about scrapbooking, and it was especially generous of him to give it to me since he had already given me a book about pirates at my other party. But I was starting to feel . . . well, I couldn't help comparing my dinner at Ollie's to Lexie's dinner at the Hard Rock Café.

After the cake, JBIII and his parents went home, and Mom set a little pile of presents on the couch in the fam-ily room. None of the packages looked like it was the right size for an iPod or a hamster environment, and since they were all wrapped, I knew none of them contained a living hamster either.

I was right. Lexie had gotten me a bottle of glittery nail polish, and Mom and Dad had gotten me a hair clip with fake rubies on it and a pair of sunglasses for camp and a pair of jeans, which had probably come from our trip to BuyMore-PayLess. Then Daddy Bo gave me five dollars, which was good since I realized I would have to start saving for the hamster and the iPod myself.

I tucked the money into my pocket and I was just starting to feel tears in my eyes, when I glanced up and saw Mom and Dad looking at me hopefully. I remem-bered my father's face the day he had come home and told us he'd been fired from his economics job. And I thought about the fact that Mom and Dad hadn't wanted to give up our Subaru or start taking the subway to

Brooklyn to shop at BuyMore-PayLess. But they had done both things anyway.

So I swallowed hard and smiled and said, "Thank you! These are great. I think I'll go write in my scrapbook now."

The next afternoon our phone rang. Dad answered it and said, "Yes? . . . Yes? . . . Oh, okay." And then he listened for a long time. Finally he said, "Certainly. Thank you. I'll talk to her about it and get right back to you."

"Talk to who?" I said the second he hung up. I was lounging on the couch with Bitey and a bowl of corn chips.

"To Lexie," Dad replied. "That was Mrs. Fulton from Camp Merrimac." (Mrs. Fulton is the camp director.) He leaned into the hallway and said, "Lexie?"

The screeching of my sister's violin came to a stop and Lexie appeared in the family room. "Yeah?"

"Mrs. Fulton just called. She has an offer for us. Well, really for you. It turns out that there's an unexpected shortage of CITs this summer." (In case you don't know it, a CIT is a counselor-in-training—a cross between a counselor and a camper since you get to be both, but you have to be at least thirteen.) "Mrs. Fulton said you can attend camp for free," Dad continued, "if you'll agree to be a CIT for one of the younger groups for half of each day. In the mornings you can be with your friends. What do you think?" Dad looked hopeful again, like he had the night before when I'd unwrapped my hair clip and sunglasses.

I could tell that Lexie didn't think much of the idea at all. And who could blame her? She had to hang out with me when she was at home. Why would she want to hang out with a whole bunch of me's every afternoon at camp?

Lexie pursed her lips like an old person. But then she smiled and said, "Sure. That would be great." And she disappeared back down the hall.

II. I went to Camp Merrimac, which is a day camp.

   A. Lexie was a CIT for my troop.

One sad thing about day camp is that the mornings start off a lot like school mornings. You have to get up early, eat a big breakfast because the only food you'll get before lunch is a camp snack such as trail mix, which is like bird food for people, remember to put a lot of stuff in your backpack (for instance, sunblock and extra underwear), and then hurry out the door so that you don't miss the camp bus, which looks exactly like a school bus. This summer it was especially important not to miss the bus because if we did, how would Lexie and I get to New Jersey without the green Subaru for backup? We missed the bus once last summer and Mom just got the

Subaru out of the garage and drove us to New Jersey saying, "The perfect day for an adventure! Plus, I have writer's block."

"Do you have everything?" Mom called as Dad and Lexie and I were stepping into the elevator on the first morning of camp. She asks us this every single school morning and every single camp morning, and I always say yes without thinking.

Lexie usually pauses to consider first. This morning she asked, "Are you *positive* there's a no-electronics rule at camp?" even though she knew the answer, since there has always been a no-electronics rule at Camp Merrimac. Lexie just couldn't stand the idea of being out of sight of her cell phone. It's possible she's forgotten what it's like to be a person who doesn't have one at all. A person such as, oh, *me.*

"I'm positive," said Mom. "Have fun." She closed the door to our apartment.

Now Lexie turned to Dad. "You really don't have to walk with us," she said. "*Really.* We're going less than three blocks."

"I want to meet the bus driver," said Dad, "and make sure where the bus stop is."

"Isn't it at the same corner where we got the bus last summer?" asked Lexie. "Sixth and Fourteenth?"

I began to hum. The doors opened, I ran into the

lobby, called hi to John at the desk, ran on outside, and met up with JBIII. We walked ahead of Dad and Lexie so as to be out of earshot of my sister's arguments, and we were one half of one block from the bus stop when I came to a halt so fast that a lady behind us ran into me and stepped on my heel.

"What's the matter?" asked JBIII as the lady rushed by us, glaring at me and not apologizing.

I pointed to the bus stop. "Look who's there," I wailed.

JBIII sucked in his breath. Then he let it out slowly. "Jill," he whispered.

I had thought Jill was out of my hair for the summer. "She didn't say anything about Camp Merrimac on the last day of school," I whined, but very quietly so as not to attract Jill's attention.

"Well," said JBIII, and I knew he was remembering what I *had* talked about—cowboys and stallions and panning for gold. But it was nice of him not to mention it, and that is why he's my new best friend.

"I can't stand it!" I cried. "Not another month with Jill." It was totally unfair. First my father gets fired and now this.

"Maybe she won't be in your group," said JBIII.

That was certainly something to hope for. Camp Merrimac is big. Over two hundred kids go to it every session, and there are four troops in each age group—two troops of girls and two of boys. Jill would be in one of the 10 to 11-year-old-girl troops, and with any luck I would be in the other.

At least Jill wasn't standing independently at the bus stop. Her mother was with her.

"Hi, Mrs. DiNunzio," I said in exactly the same tone of voice I use whenever I have to greet Mrs. Mott. Then, sounding even more unhappy, I added, "Hi, Jill."

Jill gave me a big fake smile. I had a feeling it would get even bigger and faker when Justine got on the bus at 79th Street.

Lexie and JBIII and Jill and I and a few kids I didn't know waited on the corner until the Camp Merrimac bus arrived. We all got on in a hurry, ignoring our parents. I shoved JBIII into a seat on the side of the bus facing the traffic on Fourteenth Street, but then I couldn't help myself—I stood up, leaned across the aisle, and looked out at the parents. And there was Dad craning his neck, hoping to see Lexie and me, and waving at all the windows just in case we should appear in one. I glanced at JBIII, pulled him to the other side of the bus, stuck my head partway out a window, and gave my dad a tiny wave.

Dad grinned. I smiled and then pulled my head inside before the driver could yell at me. While the parents clustered at the door to the bus and spoke with the driver, JBIII and I settled into our seat. Lexie made her way to the very back of the bus and Jill sat down directly in front of me.

"Let's move," I said to JBIII, but he muttered, "What's the point? She'll probably just follow us."

I sat with my arms crossed and stared out the window until we reached 79th Street. I considered telling Jill that her hair smelled, but I thought she might take it as a compliment.

At 79th Street six kids got on the camp bus, including Justine, who ran down the aisle shouting, "Hi, Pearl! Hi, Pearl!" She almost sat next to Jill, but thought better of it and scooted into the seat behind JBIII and me.

"Hi, Justine," I said, keeping my voice low and hoping she would get the point. She didn't. She reached into her backpack, pulled out a box of animal crackers, said, "Look what I have!" at the top of her lungs, and held the box out to me. "Want one?"

I didn't want to be rude, so I took a tiger from the box and was biting its head off when I heard JBIII say, "I didn't know you were going to Camp Merrimac this summer."

I swiveled around in my seat.

"Yeah," Jill replied. "My parents thought it would be good for me. I've never been to camp before."

"Me neither."

I couldn't help myself. "Um, where are Rachel and Katie?" I asked.

A bright pink polka dot appeared on each of Jill's cheeks. "Camp Acadia," she said.

"Day camp?" JBIII wanted to know.

Jill shook her head. "Sleepaway camp. They'll be there for most of the summer."

"Look!" said Justine from behind me. "I broke a hippo head off and put it on a kangaroo. Now it's a hip-poroo!"

I patted her hand. Justine was my best friend, but I realized that she was not the same kind of best friend as JBIII was. She was my best friend in the way Bitey was my boyfriend. You needed a lot of patience. And imagination.

"So," JBIII said to Jill, "you won't see each other all summer?"

Jill shook her head.

Huh, I thought. This was interesting. No Jill-Rachel-Katie. And Jill didn't look too happy about it. She would be on her own at Camp Merrimac.

The bus rumbled along through New Jersey. The driver, who was new, got a little lost and we turned around so many times that a kid in the back barfed, and Lexie darted forward and sat next to Justine. I thought that, as a CIT, she might have helped the kid, but Lexie is not fond of throw-up, her own or anyone else's.

When we finally drove through the gates of Camp

Merrimac we were only fifteen minutes late and everyone was still getting organized. I hopped off the bus. "Stick with me," I said to JBIII. "I'll show you what to do. First we have to get assigned to our groups."

We walked across a grassy field with Lexie and Justine. Beyond the edges of the field were all the familiar things I remembered from other summers—the softball diamond, the arts and crafts cabin, the path to the lake with its docks and canoes, the rec hall for rainy days, the playground for the youngest campers, the outdoor performance stage, and the cabins where the older campers got to stay if they signed up for a week of overnight camp. FYI, Lexie and JBIII and I were going to stay overnight for the whole last week of camp. It would be my first time.

I smiled at JBIII. All around us were trees and flowers and the sounds of birds and frogs. I hoped JBIII would like New Jersey as much as I did.

"Ooh!" cried Lexie suddenly, pointing above our heads as a great gray bird flew low over the trees. "That's a heron."

"Really?" said Justine. "I thought it was a pterodactyl."

We had joined a mob of kids who were laughing and talking and jumping up to make fake baskets in the air. I breathed in deeply. This was *so* much better than school.

"All right, listen up!" called a counselor who was

holding a clipboard. "I'm going to call out the names of the counselors, followed by the names of the campers in each group. Please join your group as soon as you hear your name."

It took a long time, but eventually Justine had joined one of the 8- to 9-year-old-girl groups and JBIII had joined one of the 10- to 11-year-old-boy groups and now it was time to assign the 10- to 11-year-old-girl groups. I squeezed my eyes shut and crossed my fingers. At last I heard, "Lisa Anderson, Pearl Littlefield." The very next thing I heard was, "Lisa Anderson, Jill DiNunzio."

I sent a furious look in JBIII's direction, but he was too far away to see it. I turned and tromped across the field toward Lisa. Jill hurried after me.

Lisa smiled at us as we approached. She was already surrounded by nine other girls. "You must be Pearl and Jill," she said. "Okay. We just need one more—oh, here she comes. Are you Deanna?"

"Yes," said a freckle-faced girl.

"Great. That's everyone. Welcome to our troop. We'll give ourselves a name later. But let's start with some introductions. I'm Lisa, and I'll be your head counselor." I didn't remember Lisa from other summers, but I decided I liked her. She smiled a lot and was wearing a T-shirt that said WHO CARES? in bold red letters across the front. "And this," Lisa continued, "is Janie. She's your junior counselor. We're also going to have two CITs—one in the morning and one in the afternoon. This is your morning CIT, Cathy."

"Call me Cat." A very perky girl who was Lexie's age waved around at us campers like she was a celebrity, which she was not, since she was unfortunately wearing a T-shirt with a picture of a little-girl cat in a frilly dress and pink party shoes sipping tea from a cup that said KITTEA under the rim.

Jill took one look at the shirt and snorted. She snorted loudly enough for everyone in our troop to hear, and they all looked at her, and Janie frowned. I think Janie was going to say something about considering people's feelings and not snorting, but at that moment I caught sight of Lexie, and the next thing I knew Lisa was nudging her forward and announcing, "And this is Lexie, your afternoon CIT."

My eyes shot themselves over to Lexie whose own eyes were bugging out of their sockets. Lexie was going to be *my* CIT? I didn't have to be a mind reader to know that at that exact same second Lexie was thinking, I have to be *Pearl's* CIT?

The God of Unfairness was working overtime.

I paused to think about how a mature person would handle the situation.

I raised my hand.

"We're not in *school*," Jill whispered loudly, and snorted again.

"Yes, Pearl?" said Lisa.

"May I please switch into another group?" I asked in my politest voice. This would get me away from both Jill and Lexie, which would solve two problems at once, which seemed very efficient.

"Pearl!" exclaimed Lexie, and her face turned red but maybe everyone would just think it was sunburn.

"No switching groups until after we've given them a fair try," Lisa replied pleasantly.

Jill started to snort for a third time but cut it short because no one joined in with her, and two girls, who I think were eleven because they were wearing bras (you could see the white straps next to the straps of their tank tops), looked at each other and did eye rolls.

Jill noticed this and her polka dots came back.

"Thank you for considering my request," I said courteously to Lisa.

Lexie left then to join her own group for the morning, and Lisa led the rest of us to a large tree, which I don't know what kind it was but it was still very pretty except for some bird poop. We sat down under it, avoiding the poop. Jill tried to sit next to the bra girls but they got up and moved so then Jill plunked down next to me.

"First order of business . . . ," said Lisa, and she began to tell us about Camp Merrimac and camp rules and where the bathrooms are and what time lunch is and blah, blah, blahdy-blah, blah. The only part I listened to was the list of art activities like ceramics and beading.

After that we all went around and said our names. Three of the ten-year-olds had been at Camp Merrimac the summer before, and we gave each other high fives even though we didn't really know each other since I hadn't been in their troop.

No one wanted to high-five Jill. I tried not to feel sorry about this, but I sort of did.

When we had finished saying our names I realized that the only ones I remembered were Jill's, Lisa's, Cat's (because of her T-shirt), and my own. So it was good that the next thing Lisa said was, "Our second order of business is to make name tags."

We sat down at a picnic table and got to work with a box of art supplies. Here is some info about the girls in my troop:

Name	Age	Comments, if any
Deanna	10	Freckles
Eliza	10	Has already cried twice
Misty	10	Best friends with Deanna
Vonna	10	Screamed at sight of ant
Sherry	11	Bra Girl #1
Janelle	11	Bra Girl #2
Juwanna	11	Wants to be a painter
Mary Grace	11	Will not stop talking
Lena	11	Opposite of Mary Grace
Denise	11	Says she has a boyfriend
Jill	10	----------
Me	10	NA, which means not applicable, since I already know myself
Lisa	21	Head counselor
Janie	17	Junior counselor
Cat	14	Morning CIT, weird kit-tea shirt
Lexie	14	Afternoon CIT, blah, blah, blah

"Be sure to leave the bottom half of your name tag blank," Lisa said as we worked away, "because we need to think up a name for our troop, and you'll add that under your own name."

"I know what we should call ourselves," said Mary Grace. "The Jersey Girls!"

"But I'm from New York," said Jill, which, hello, so am I, but of course Jill did not mention that, since the only person who is important to her is herself.

"How about the Merrymakers?" said Vonna. "You know, because we're at Camp Merrimac?"

Jill frowned at her.

"The Kitties?" suggested Cat.

"Well . . . maybe," said Lena kindly.

"I have an idea," I said, which I would never have done if this was school, and Rachel and Katie were around to back Jill up. "How about the Starlettes?"

There was silence. Then Bra Girl #1 said, "Ooh, I like the sound of that!"

"Me, too," said Denise. "Especially since I'm going to be a star someday."

"I like it, too," said Deanna.

"Let's take a vote," said Lisa. "All those in favor of the Starlettes, raise your hand."

I looked around at a forest of raised hands.

"Anyone not in favor?"

Jill shot her hand in the air like a person who expects

every single cab on the street to pull over and stop for her whether they're already occupied or not. The Bra Girls rolled their eyes again.

"Okay. We are officially the Starlettes," said Lisa.

And we all wrote THE STARLETTES on our name tags.

After that we finally got around to some real camp activities. We changed into our bathing suits and swam in the lake. I must point out that while I don't mind wearing nothing but my underwear in front of Lexie, I'm not fond of changing in front of a bunch of other people, even if they are girls. For instance, I didn't want Jill to see my pink underwear, in case she thought it was babyish. I spent a lot of time trying to figure out if I could put my bathing suit on over the underpants and then whisk the panties out from under the suit like a magician, but this turned out to be impossible, and also it made me fall down. Finally, I tied a beach towel around me and managed to change inside it, like a tent. I noticed the Bra Girls doing the same thing, except that something told me they sort of wanted us ten-year-olds to see their bosoms.

After our swim we had to endure changing again, except in reverse, but after that, we played volleyball. And then it was time for lunch. Everyone gathered at the picnic tables in the field. I waved to Justine, who was eating with her group, and then I sat down next to JBIII.

"I saw a snake," he said, and I wasn't sure whether he thought that was good or bad.

"I named my troop," I replied, and pointed to my name tag.

JBIII's troop was called the Dudes.

"I'm going to try canoeing this afternoon," he said.

"I signed up for ceramics class." I paused. Then I asked my best friend, "How do you like Camp Merrimac?"

"So far so good."

II. I went to Camp Merrimac, which is a day camp.

  A. Lexie was a CIT for my troop.

  B. Camp was fun even though Lexie was my CIT, and even though one of the Starlettes was Jill DiNunzio.

I was having so much fun being a Starlette at Camp Merrimac that I had completely forgotten that the afternoon would bring a bad thing—the ball of boringness known as Lexie. The moment lunch was over, Lexie joined the Starlettes as our afternoon CIT.

She started off trying to be all cool and grown-up, even though by next summer the eleven-year-old Starlettes would be old enough to be in the group Lexie was in now, which, FYI, the kids in my sister's group had named themselves the Rock and Roll Girls, even though not one of them could sing, including Lexie, plus I don't know too many rock-and-roll violinists.

Lexie strode over to the Starlettes just as we were cleaning up our lunch stuff. "So, what's on the docket for the afternoon?" she asked Lisa, clapping her hands together earnestly. She completely ignored Janie, since Janie was just the junior counselor, not the head counselor, and if there's anything Lexie likes it's people who are in charge, such as school principals, mayors, and orchestra conductors.

Lisa looked a teensy bit surprised. "On the docket?" she repeated. "Oh, I see. Well, next is free time, followed by Sign-up Activities One and then Sign-up Activities Two. Each of the activities is an hour long. By then it will be four o'clock, and time for Camp Merrimac Cheering, which, as you know, all the campers and counselors participate in before the buses arrive."

"So," said Lexie again, and she pulled a little notebook out of her shorts pocket, "what are your expectations for me?"

I was glad that only about four of the Starlettes were listening to this conversation. I was also glad that we hadn't written our last names on our tags. Maybe no one would realize Lexie was my sister.

Jill snapped her gum in my ear. "Hey, how come your sister is our CIT?" she asked loudly. "Is it so she can help out in case, you know, you wet your pants?" She stared off into space then and began singing softly, "Tinkle, tinkle, little star . . ."

"No," I replied. "It's so she can help out in case you start to barf and can't make it to the bathroom. No one wants to see that again." If that actually did happen, Jill would die from embarrassment, and Lexie would die from seeing barf. The Bra Girls were standing nearby. "Did you know," I said to them, "that Jill and I go to the same school, and one time Jill had to barf and she didn't—"

Jill yanked me away just as Lisa announced, "Okay, everyone, free time! Your choices are hiking, softball, arts and crafts, and canoeing. Tell me where you're going to be for the next hour."

"Canoeing!" I cried. Sadly, this was before Lisa assigned Lexie to the canoeing group.

I stayed ten paces behind Lexie as she tried to walk through the woods and scribble in her CIT notebook at the same time. Lisa had told her that her only duties were to help out and to enforce the rules of the lake. This shouldn't have taken very long to write down, which probably meant that Lexie was making up extra rules of her own.

We tromped along a path, and I saw a couple of squirrels and a chipmunk, plus some bugs and a newt. When I saw the newt I knew we were near the water. I squinted ahead, and sure enough, there was the lake, shining in the sunlight.

Behind me, Juwanna and Eliza started to run. They ran past me and onto the main dock, and the second their feet touched the wooden boards I heard someone shout, "No running on the docks!" which is the very first rule on the giant sign that's posted on the back of the life-guard stand.

Of course the shouter was Lexie. She was pleased to be able to show off her CIT bossing skills.

Juwanna and Eliza came to a screeching stop and Ju-wanna tripped over a little boy and Eliza started to cry.

Lexie strode toward them. She looked confused when she realized that Juwanna was the one who had tripped, but Eliza was the one who was crying.

I hopped onto the dock behind Lexie, tugged at her shirt, and whispered loudly, "You made Eliza cry!"

"What?" Lexie whispered back, frowning.

"You yelled at her. She cries at everything."

Lexie hesitated, but she couldn't help herself. "You broke a rule," she said to Eliza. Then she turned to Ju-wanna. "You, too . . ."—she peered at her name tag—"Juwanna."

"Sorry," said Juwanna, who was already halfway down the dock, heading for the canoes.

Eliza sniffled sadly and wiped at her tears. "I forgot," she said. "I haven't been here since last summer."

Lexie patted her shoulder. "That's okay. But maybe we should review the rules together," she said, leading her toward the lifeguard stand. "You, too, Pearl."

"Me? I didn't do anything."

"Rules are always helpful. Now, read with me."

In our dullest, most humiliated voices, Eliza and I read the list of rules aloud with Lexie. "No running on the docks. No one permitted on the docks unless a counselor is present. No swimming unless the lifeguard is present. No horseplay . . ."

We read down to the final rule and Eliza and Lexie stopped speaking, but I continued, "No having fun. No naked swimming. No swimming if your sister is present. No—" I glanced at Eliza who was giggling, and at Lexie who was giving me the Evil Sister Eye.

Then Lexie turned and stalked off to see if she could humiliate anyone else.

At least Jill wasn't around. She had decided to play softball, and I had decided that from now on I would always wait to see what Jill picked during free time and then I would pick something else.

Lexie climbed into a canoe with poor Eliza and a junior counselor, and then I got in a canoe with Juwanna and some counselor I didn't know and we paddled all around the lake and the counselor identified birdcalls while Juwanna told me she has a brother who goes to college and sends her funny animal photos in e-mail, which obviously means that Juwanna has her own personal computer. But she wasn't snobby about it.

When free time was over Lexie led Juwanna and Eliza and me back through the woods to meet up with the other Starlettes. We had reached the field and were walking by the softball diamond when we heard the crack of a bat and almost instantly we also heard someone shriek and then I saw Lena (the non-talking Starlette) grab her leg and fall on the ground. This didn't look fake at all, and I realized that the kid who had just hit the ball had thrown the bat to the side, which it had accidentally whacked Lena on the shin.

"Ow!" she wailed. "Ow, ow, *ow*!"

My sister ran to Lena and took a look at her leg. I was right behind Lexie, and I could see a lump already forming on Lena's shin.

"Oh, it hurts," Lena whispered, which was somehow more frightening than her shrieking. She hunched over her leg and started to cry quietly.

"Move back!" Lexie said to the kids who had crowded around. "Give us some space. Can somebody please go get the nurse? Tell her to bring the ice pack. The stretcher, too, just in case."

I stared at my sister. Lexie looked completely calm and not scared, which was the opposite of how I felt.

"I think it's broken," said Lena in that same small voice. "What if it's broken?"

"You're going to be fine," was Lexie's reply, and she sat down next to Lena and let her rest against her shoulder. I remembered last Thanksgiving when I had eaten too much at dinner and had woken up during the night with a stomachache and Lexie had been very soothing and nice to me even though there was the danger of barf.

"Are you sure it isn't broken?" Lena asked again.

"Stand her up," suggested one of the junior counselors. "See if she can walk on it."

Lexie shook her head. "No. We should wait for the nurse," she said firmly.

The nurse came hurrying across the field then with a bag of supplies, followed by two junior counselors with a stretcher.

It turned out that Lena's leg was not broken, just badly bruised. She limped off the field, the nurse on one side of her, Lexie on the other. As they walked by me I heard the nurse say, "Good job, Lexie. You did everything right," and all my sister said was, "Thank you," not "I know," or "I've had training" (which she hadn't), or anything stuck up.

"Lexie is my sister!" I called after the nurse, who didn't hear me. Lexie did, though, and she turned and gave me a smile.

— * —

When all the excitement had died down it was time for sign-up activities. I had signed up for a ceramics class and Sock Monkey Animals, which really could just have been called Sock Animals since monkeys *are* animals, but whatever. In ceramics we made some beads for jewelry and got introduced to the potter's wheels we'd use later when we were more experienced. In Sock Monkey Animals I found out that you can make any kind of animal out of any kind of sock, not just monkeys out of the brown and red and white socks, so I started working on a blue-and-white-striped dog that I thought maybe I would give Dad to make him feel better.

It was my kind of afternoon, with crafts galore, and I couldn't wait for the next day of camp. Plus, I decided I didn't need to switch out of the Starlettes after all. Having Lexie for my CIT wasn't so bad, and I thought I could put up with Jill. I made the decision *after* the incident at the end of the day, which says a lot about how mature I've become.

The incident took place during Camp Merrimac Cheering. Cheering is fun because no one says, "Indoor voice, Pearl," since you are ex*pect*ed to cheer at top volume. We were all chanting, "Cumila, cumila, cumila vista; oh, no no not la vista; Eenie-meeny docile-eeny; ooh, ah, walla-weenie . . ." which is my favorite chant because it gets faster and faster and then at the end you get to yell, "Yee-haw!"

We were winding up for the yee-haw, when I glanced at Jill, who unfortunately was standing right next to me since the Bra Girls and most of the other Starlettes had no interest in her whatsoever, and I saw that she wasn't chanting. Since she hadn't been to Camp Merrimac before she didn't know about eenie-meeny docile-eeny and probably felt on the outskirts of things like I used to feel at Emily Dickinson Elementary before I got JBIII for my best friend.

So anyway Jill and I were standing shoulder to shoulder and I was shouting, "Ish biddly oten-doten; bo-bo and ditten-datten!" when I felt soft breath in my ear and realized Jill was saying something to me. Of course, I couldn't hear her. I brushed her away like a fly. "Yee-haw!" I cried along with the rest of Camp Merrimac, and thought—just briefly—of cowboys shouting "Yee-haw!" as they rode by cactuses and buzzards in the deserts of the Wild West.

I looked at Jill. "What did you say?"

"Oh," she replied, twisting her finger around a strand of hair, "I was just remembering a field trip we went on once." She raised her voice so that the Bra Girls would be in hearing range. "It seems to me that something happened. What was it? Oh, yes. Someone in our grade got lost. Why . . . it was you! And instead of looking for your teacher you stood there and yelled, 'Help, police!'"

The Bra Girls began to laugh.

I could tell that Jill was getting geared up to continue her story when, just like in fairy tales, a shadow suddenly fell across her face.

It was Lexie's shadow, and my sister was glaring at Jill with cool snake eyes.

"Lexie, don't—," I started to say.

But my sister ignored me. "You know, Jill. Maybe you could let go of that incident. It happened when you guys were in *third grade*. You seem pretty clever to me. I'm sure you could come up with a new insult now that you're going into fifth grade."

"Hey!" I exclaimed. "What do you mean, a new insult?" But then I saw that the polka dots were reappearing on Jill's cheeks. And that now the Bra Girls were laughing at *her*. She turned away and slithered into a group of tall kids, and I didn't see her again until we climbed onto the bus. JBIII sat with me and Lexie plopped down next to Justine, who was right in back of me. I have to say that Justine had looked a little sad when she'd gotten on the bus and found JBIII already sitting next to me, but I forgot about that when Jill climbed aboard. This was because the second Jill saw Lexie, she and her polka dots hurried all the way to the back of the bus.

"So," I said to him, "do you like camp?" I had only seen him at lunch. I had tried to get him to go to Sock

Monkey Animals, but instead he had signed up for a class called Write Right for kids who want to be authors, which is not me.

"Yeah," he replied. "It's cool."

"I can teach you the chants," I added, since I suddenly realized he must have been in the same boat as Jill during Camp Merrimac Cheering.

JBIII and Justine and Lexie and I spent most of the ride chanting "Cumila, cumila" (which cheered Justine up) and not looking at the back of the bus, where Jill was sitting with a bunch of kids she didn't know. When the driver finally pulled up at the corner of 6th Avenue and 14th Street, Lexie and JBIII and I rushed down the steps and onto the sidewalk, hoping to get a head start and avoid Jill.

I crashed into someone. It was my father. He looked sort of tired, but he put on a big smile when he saw us.

"Hi!" he said. "How was camp? I thought I'd walk you home."

"But Lexie is here," I replied. The other kids at our stop were either walking home by themselves or being met by baby-sitters. Dad was the only fired parent who had shown up.

Lexie glared at me and said, "Thanks, Dad," which I guess she had forgotten the fit she had had in the morning when Dad walked us *to* the bus stop. No matter how mature I get, she is always maturer.

That night I sat at my desk, found a piece of deep blue paper the color of the lake at camp, and wrote (keeping in mind that Mom and Dad would probably want to look through my scrapbook at the end of the summer): First day of camp it was fun, even what with Jill DiNunzio. Am making a sock dog! (I figured that by the time Dad saw the scrapbook he would already be the owner of the sock dog.) Lexie is my afternoon CIT and very skilled at first aid. Can't wait for tomorrow. I thought for a moment, then added: Thank you, Mom and Dad.

I glued the paper onto a scrapbook page and decorated the edges of the page with drawings of roses, leaves, newts, and Lena getting whacked by the bat.

II. I went to Camp Merrimac, which is a day camp.

   A. Lexie was a CIT for my troop.

   B. Camp was fun even though Lexie was my CIT, and even though one of the Starlettes was Jill DiNunzio.

   C. JBIII and I starred in a talent show.

The rest of the first week of camp was mostly good, with only a few unfortunate things thrown in:

What Happened	Good	Bad
Cook-out with hotdogs		X
Almost finished sock dog	X	
Lake evacuated due to water snake		X
Jill lost bathing-suit top while swimming		X
Lexie made Bra Girl #2 recite lake rules	X	
Lexie saved Starlettes from nest of hornets	X	
Saw boy counselor and girl counselor kissing	X	X
Jill pestered JBIII		X
Scared Jill with nonexistent spider		X
Talent show announced for Friday	X	

I thought I had Jill under control, but I guess I didn't. No matter how many times I stared at her with the cool snake eyes that Lexie had perfected, Jill would not leave JBIII alone. She kept trying to talk to him. She would be all, "Jamie"—that's what she called him—"what are you doing for free time this afternoon?" and "Oh, Jamie, I love your Write Right story," and "Here, have half my sandwich, Jamie." Once when we were getting on the bus at the end of the day, Justine slid in next to me and Jill tried to slide in next to JBIII, but he swiveled his head around like an owl and looked at me with hysteria eyes that called "Save me!" so I rescued him by shoving Justine onto the seat across the aisle and saying, "JBThree, come help me with this," even though I was just sitting there and didn't need help with anything. Justine looked wounded, and I whispered, "Sorry, sorry. I'll explain later," which was pointless because one thing Justine doesn't understand is what it's like to be ten.

Then JBIII scrambled over Jill's knees, whooshed down next to me, and rolled his eyes. I think Jill saw this, but even so, she said, "Want to play tennis tomorrow, Jamie?" and then JBIII was just like, "*No*," so finally Jill faced forward.

The next day I caught Jill watching JBIII and me on the bus. Then I saw her looking at JBIII in his swimming trunks while he was canoeing. When I realized that she was eavesdropping on us during lunch I said to JBIII, "Hey, I think there's a spider crawling up Jill's—"

I hadn't even finished the sentence before Jill scrambled to her feet and began hopping up and down, shaking her shirt out, brushing at her legs (which, sorry for being gross, are on the hairy side), and whiffling her hands through her ponytails. "Where is it? Where is it?" she shrieked.

"Where's what?" asked Cat, who was wearing the Kit-Tea shirt again.

"The spider!"

"I don't see any spider." Cat got to her feet and turned Jill around a few times like she was a display rack at BuyMore-PayLess.

"There's a spider?" screamed Vonna, and then she was on her feet, too. Vonna likes spiders even less than ants, and she really doesn't belong at an outdoor day camp, if you ask me.

"Are you sure there's no spider?" Jill said to Cat. She was breathing heavily and her polka dots had returned and her hair looked like a bird's nest and all in all she wasn't very attractive to boys or anyone else at that particular second.

"Positive," Cat replied, but since by then she had sat down and was pawing through her lunch again, Jill didn't believe her. She kept holding her arms out and turning them over, and peering down the backs of her legs, and finally she borrowed someone's comb and ran it through her ponytails and shook her head like Bitey shakes his when he has ear mites.

So then I said to JBIII, "I wonder if young girls can get ear mites," and Jill glared at me and I felt satisfied.

This was on Friday, and it was one of the good things that happened that week, but the very best thing happened a few hours later at Camp Cheering. We had just finished chanting "X Marks the Spot" and giving each other the shivers when Edward, who's the counselor in charge of drama, stood up in front of the whole camp and said, "Here's something fun to think about over the weekend: Next Friday—that's a week from today—we're going to have a talent showcase in the afternoon. Anyone can sign up for it, and any kind of talent is welcome. Just let me know by the end of the day on Monday if you want to participate."

Jill launched her hand in the air like a rocket. "Will there be prizes?" she asked, which I'm sure she was picturing herself being awarded a gold trophy even though her talent is limited to Hair Styling.

Edward smiled. "Nope," he said. "No prizes, no judging. This is just for fun. You can sign up by yourself or with a friend or you can put together a group."

Jill pouted. She likes winners and losers. Even so, I saw her heading toward JBIII and I knew what she was going to ask him, so before she could snare my best friend I grabbed his arm and said, "Let's sing a duet in the show." (The important word in that sentence is "duet"—as in *two* people.)

JBIII looked a little surprised. "I don't think I'm a very good si—"

"Great!" I said. "We'll work on it over the weekend."

Jill swished up to us then, all breathy like a movie star. "Jamie!" she cried. "Let's put together an act for the talent show."

"Oh, he can't," I told her. "We're going to sing a duet. We just decided. Maybe you could do a solo act," I added brightly.

"Oh," said Jill. "Well, maybe."

JBIII and I got busy that weekend.

"We don't have much time to rehearse," I said to him. It was Saturday morning and JBIII and I were sitting on my bedroom floor.

"We don't even know what we're going to sing," JBIII replied, edging away from Bitey and looking a little nervous. But I couldn't tell if he was nervous about singing in front of two hundred kids or nervous about being bitten.

"Yes, we do. I mean, I do. I thought of the perfect song. It's called 'Friendship'—since we're such good friends."

It was a song I knew all too well. Lexie has decided that one day she's going to play her violin in a Broadway orchestra, so she listens to musicals endlessly in her room and tries to play her violin along with the songs.

One show she has listened to about ten bazillion times is called *Anything Goes* and that's where I'd heard the friendship song.

"Now there are a lot of verses in the song," I said.

"Long verses?" asked JBIII, looking even more nervous.

"Sort of. That's why I think we should only sing two of them."

JBIII let out his breath. "Okay. Good. Two verses. Write down the words so I can practice at home."

"Write them down?" I said, and a little whine came into my voice. "Let me sing them for you first." I stood up, grabbed the stapler from my desk, and held it to my mouth. "If you're ever up a tree, phone to me," I sang loudly. "If you're ever down a well, ring my bell." I stopped. "Hey, I just had a great idea. When I say 'phone to me' you should pick up a phone. And when I say 'ring my bell' you should ring a bell."

"You mean I don't have to sing?" asked JBIII hopefully.

"No, we both have to sing."

"Then please write down the words."

As you can see, we disagreed a little about our song, and eventually we got tired of rehearsing so we decided to practice tripping instead. "You have to make it look real," I told JBIII. "Like this." I walked into the family room, caught my foot on the edge of the rug, and crashed into Dad's fax machine. JBIII laughed. Then he pretended to fall over Bitey. He landed on the couch, boinged into an armchair, and almost accidentally landed on Bitey for real.

"What are you doing?" asked Lexie from behind us. She looked horrified, like she had discovered us eating caterpillars.

"Practicing," I told her.

"That's what you're going to do in the talent show?"

"No, for the show we're going to sing 'Friendship.'"

Lexie perked up. "From *Anything Goes*?"

JBIII nodded.

"Want me to help you?"

That was how Lexie appointed herself our talent coach and JBIII and I wound up rehearsing way more than we had meant to, even after Lexie politely mentioned that neither of us could carry a tune.

"Are you sure you want to go through with this?" she asked us on the following Thursday, the afternoon before the show. Camp was over for the day and Lexie had insisted that JBIII and I have one more rehearsal. Dad was our audience, sitting on the couch in the office/family room and looking at us fondly, since fathers always have to think everything their children do is wonderful even when the children can't carry a tune.

"Yes," I said.

And JBIII whispered to me, "Do we have to sing in front of your father?" He may have forgotten that the next day he would be singing in front of the entire camp.

"Yes," I said again.

JBIII and I hooked arms and began to take side steps across the family room. This was what Lexie called choreography, and she said a dance routine was especially important for JBIII and me so that the audience would focus on what we were doing instead of on the sound of our voices. Also, for some reason, she had recommended that we do away with the telephone and the bell.

We began the song. "If you're ever up a tree, phone to me!"

We mixed up two lines, and JBIII lost track of the tune and just shouted the words instead, but all in all I thought we did a pretty good job. When we finished, Lexie shook her head and put her hand over her eyes, but my father jumped to his feet and shouted, "Bravo!" and I imagined that we would get another standing ovation the next day.

It turned out that an awful lot of kids had signed up for the talent show. Edward got things going at 1:30, hoping the show would be over by 4:00, which was a very long time to sit outside on log benches, especially for the youngest kids, and quite a few of them wandered away to use the bathroom or get trail mix, and one kid went after a squirrel and never came back to his bench, so the audience kept getting smaller and smaller. JBIII and I sat together with our talent coach, Lexie Littlefield. We watched kids sing solos and duets and recite poems and tap-dance and do hip-hop and put on skits. We watched kids play flutes and guitars and clarinets.

"Hey," JBIII whispered to Lexie, "how come you didn't want to play your violin?"

My sister shook her head. She has a problem with performance, which I certainly hope she gets over by the time she's playing in a Broadway orchestra.

Lena and Mary Grace presented a rap song they had written, which was pretty good until the end when they couldn't find anything to rhyme with "Merrimac."

Then Jill walked onto the stage. She was in the middle of doing a cheerleading routine without pom-poms when I felt someone tap my back.

I turned around.

Dad was sitting behind us. He was the only parent who had shown up. This was because parents hadn't been invited.

I gasped and nudged Lexie. She turned around, too. "Dad!" she exclaimed. "What are you doing?"

"I wanted to see the talent show," he said.

"How did you get here?" I asked.

Dad held his finger to his lips. "I'll tell you later. I didn't miss your number, did I?"

And at that very second I heard a thin little applause for Jill, and then Edward announced, "Next up are Pearl Littlefield and James Brubaker."

I don't think you'll be very surprised to find out that "Friendship" didn't go much better at camp than it had in our family room the day before. JBIII forgot the words of the first verse entirely, and the dance steps, too, so for a while he just stood on the stage and watched me, and I'm pretty sure I didn't have the tune right because when I looked out into the audience I saw Lexie with her head in her hands. Toward the end of our number I stepped on JBIII's foot and he said "Yow" and limped through the rest of the routine.

The applause for JBIII and me was even thinner than it had been for Jill—until I heard a familiar shout of "Bravo!" and saw that Dad had leaped up from his bench and was clapping hard, his hands held above his head. After his second "bravo" he cried, "Encore!" (which means you should do another verse), but luckily Lexie got him to sit down.

JBIII and I plopped onto the first row of benches, which were now empty since all the six- and seven-year-olds had gone off to eat trail mix and play games. There were five numbers left in the show, and after each one I turned around to check on Dad. He was still sitting on his bench, Lexie red-faced in front of him. He stayed during Camp Merrimac Cheering, too, and I realized that he had memorized "Cumila, cumila, cumila vista," and when we shouted "Yee-haw!" I could hear Dad's voice over everyone else's.

Another thing that happened that afternoon was that all the Starlettes and all the Rock and Roll Girls kept staring at Dad and giggling.

At last the buses got fired up, and it was time to leave. That was when my father ran to Lexie and JBIII and me (he was wearing sneakers) and said he was going to drive us home.

"In what?" I asked.

"Mrs. Mott's car."

"You borrowed Mrs. Mott's car?" said Lexie, just as I said, "Mrs. Mott knows how to drive?"

Mrs. Mott's car smelled like her and was the cleanest, neatest car I've ever seen. Our green Subaru used to have all sorts of things strewn around in it—water bottles and towels and maps and baseball hats and empty packages of cookies and a flashlight and a plastic shovel in case we ever got stuck in a snowbank, which seemed unlikely.

In Mrs. Mott's car were just the seats. I wanted to know if she kept gum in the glove compartment, but Dad wouldn't let Lexie open it.

I sighed. From my spot in the back, where I sat stiffly, trying not to do anything that would get Mrs. Mott's car dirty, I peered at Dad. He had seemed very happy when he'd surprised us at camp, but now I thought he looked tired, and a little sad.

"Dad?" I said.

He glanced at me in the rearview mirror and put a smile on his face. "Yes?"

I hesitated. "Nothing."

III. My self-portrait (*Pearl Littlefield at Ten*) was in an art exhibit.

Going on bug hunts and making sock animals and scaring Jill might not have been as much fun as riding the range or sleeping under the stars or eating baked beans around a campfire in the desert (which, I only like the *idea* of baked beans), but it was better than nothing. And when I looked back through my scrapbook I saw that so far my summer hadn't been bad, considering I was the daughter of a fired person.

I had devoted two entire pages to the day Jill lost her bathing-suit top in the lake, and there was another page about the water snake, and one about the counselors who kissed, and another about the talent show. On the

talent-show page I even put in the part about Dad showing up and driving us home in Mrs. Mott's clean car.

Also, Mom and Dad had started talking about taking
a staycation in August. In case you're wondering what a
staycation is, it's something parents tell their kids they'll
be going on when they can't fly them out to the Wild
West after all.

"I'm going to take a whole week off from writing,"
said Mom at dinner one night as I sat hunched over my
plate on the floor of the family room. I had started out
eating at Dad's desk and had immediately dripped to-
mato sauce down the paper feed of the fax machine, so
had been banished to the floor with a stack of dish
towels.

"We'll stay in New York and do all sorts of fun things," said Dad as he swiped at the paper feed with his napkin. "We'll go to the Statue of Liberty."

"And walk across the Brooklyn Bridge," added my mother.

"Oh!" said Dad. "And—"

But luckily he was interrupted by the telephone, which Lexie jumped up to answer, even though she has her own phone, but I guess when you're her age you like to answer *all* the phones.

She listened for a couple of moments and then she said, "Okay, sure," and handed the phone to me.

It was Daddy Bo calling, and guess what, it turned out that there was something special coming up at The Towers—Grandparents' Day. All the old people who lived at The Towers could invite a grandkid (or some other relative or a friend) for an afternoon of fun. And if you were older than twelve you weren't invited, so for once there was an advantage to being younger than Lexie.

"We'll have lunch and play games and go out for ice cream *and*," Daddy Bo went on, "this is the part that I thought you'd be most interested in, Pearl—there's going to be an art exhibit for the kids. If you submit a piece of work, it'll be framed and displayed in the gallery at The Towers. And there'll be an opening reception in the gallery at the end of Grandparents' Day."

An art show! My first real art show, with an exhibit and an opening. I imagined the blue first-prize ribbon that was certain to be awarded to my painting. I would be very modest when I saw it, just all like, "Oh, this is for *me*? Why, thank you. What a surprise. I never expected it." And then I would look at the painting hanging next to mine and say, "There are so many worthwhile pieces of art here. They all deserve awards." But I probably wouldn't mean it. After that I would go home and pin the ribbon to my lampshade and leave it there until my mother decided it was a fire hazard, and then I would move it to my bulletin board.

I thanked Daddy Bo and told him I would love to go to Grandparents' Day and he told me how to submit my art and then he talked to Mom and Dad and Lexie for a while and I tried to figure out whether Lexie was disappointed that she was too old for lunch and games at the old people's home.

After dinner I got right to work on the painting for the contest. Before I had even gotten my art supplies out I knew what I was going to paint: me. I mean, a portrait of me. It would be titled *Pearl Littlefield at Ten,* and I would paint it in black and white and gray, like a photograph.

I worked on the picture all evening until Lexie stuck her head in my room and said, "Mom wants you to go to bed." Her eyes traveled to the painting. "Hey, that's really good, Pearl."

"Thanks," I replied, and luckily stopped talking before I added, "I've never won a blue ribbon before."

I decided that I should look nice for Grandparents' Day. If I was going to win first prize in the art contest and have my picture in the paper, I didn't want to be photographed wearing my jeans and my I'M THE LITTLE SISTER T-shirt, even if Daddy Bo had given it to me. I knew better than to wear the Christmas dress again, though, and after pawing through all my drawers I finally chose a pink flowered shirt that I absolutely hate but that has no holes in it and a short pink skirt that used to belong to Lexie and would be fine as long as I remembered to tug it around my knees when I sat down.

At eleven o'clock on the morning of Grandparents' Day, Dad and I walked to 14th Street and caught the subway uptown. It was enormously hot again, and sorry about this, but our subway car was not only un–air conditioned but smelled like an old egg-salad sandwich stirred up with sweat. I sat next to my father and held my nose until he turned and gave me a look that plainly said, "Please stop doing that. You're embarrassing me."

I didn't want him to feel bad about not having our green Subaru anymore, so I stopped holding my nose and just breathed through my mouth for the next fifty blocks instead.

We got out at 79th Street and walked to The Towers, which even though it's a retirement community, I sort of wish I could live there. Inside the building, besides all the apartments, are a gift shop, a beauty parlor, a barbershop, a library, a gym, a *crafts room,* and a coffee shop plus a dining room. You can sign up to go on field trips, too, so it's sort of like day camp for old people.

Daddy Bo was waiting for us in the lobby and he said, "Pearl, my gem of a granddaughter!" when he saw me. "You're looking very fetching."

My father left then, although I think he might have wanted to stay, but since he's over twelve he wasn't allowed.

Daddy Bo took my hand. "This way to the dining room," he said.

We joined a long line of grandparents and kids. Some of the older kids were pushing their grandparents in wheelchairs, and some of the grandparents were pushing little kids in strollers. Everyone was talking and laughing, and Daddy Bo looked very happy and I began to feel excited.

The dining room was decorated with a big sign that said WELCOME TO GRANDPARENTS' DAY, and there were bunches of balloons floating around the ceiling and crayons at the tables so you could color on the paper mats.

"Look at all the food," I said.

"It's buffet style," said Daddy Bo. "Grab a plate and take whatever you want."

"Really?" This was better than leftovers night, except that there wasn't any Count Chocula.

Daddy Bo and I walked up and down a long table, and I took a little helping from almost every dish there, even though I wound up with some things I didn't recognize. Then we sat at a table with three of Daddy Bo's friends and their grandchildren.

"What an adventurous eater you are," this one old lady said to me.

And at that exact moment I opened my mouth and put something shiny into it, and the shiny thing turned out to be not only very salty but also very slimy.

Daddy Bo turned to me. "I didn't know you liked oysters, Pearl."

I choked on the oyster, which was so slippery that when I accidentally swallowed, it went all the way down in about one half of a second. I gagged and drank a lot of water, but I don't think anybody noticed because the old lady said to Daddy Bo, "Her name is Pearl and she likes oysters?" and everyone laughed, including me, even though my eyes were watering.

After that, I paid more attention to what was on my plate and stuck to things like banana slices and peanut butter and hot dogs.

When lunch was over everyone went into another room for games. We played games that weren't too hard on the old people—things like Pictionary and charades—and there weren't any prizes involved, but it was still fun.

After charades, Mrs. Means, who was the activities director at The Towers and not mean at all, said, "We have about fifteen minutes before we'll leave for the ice-cream shop. Can anyone think of another game to play?"

I raised my hand. "I could teach everyone a chant," I said, and before I knew it, Daddy Bo and Mrs. Means and Daddy Bo's friends and all the kids were shouting, "Cumila, cumila, cumila vista."

After that we took a field trip to the ice-cream shop, which was only two blocks away, and thank goodness because there were those wheelchairs and strollers to push and also some people, like Daddy Bo, were a little tottery on their feet. But we made it safely.

"What do you think?" Daddy Bo asked me as we walked inside a very air-conditioned store and saw two long tables that were clearly set up just for us.

"This is great," I said.

The shop was called Dilly's, and it sold nothing but ice cream and ice-cream cones and ice-cream sundaes and something called a Banana Boat, which served six. We all sat down at the tables and looked at the menus and I was just getting ready to order a scoop of vanilla, which is the only flavor I like, when I heard a very excited voice call, "Pearl! Pearl! Hi, Pearl!"

I turned around and there was Justine with her father.

"What are you doing here?" she cried.

"What are *you* doing here?" I asked.

"We live around the corner." Justine paused. "We come here all the time," she added importantly, and I reminded myself that Justine is only eight and probably can't help bragging.

Daddy Bo stood up and shook Mr. Lebarro's hand, and Mrs. Means invited the Lebarros to join us, and before I knew it, Justine had squeezed herself in between Daddy Bo and me and announced to the table that she was getting a dog, which wasn't exactly true since her parents had said that she could get a dog when she was ten so she had two more years to go.

When everyone had finished their ice cream, Daddy Bo told the Lebarros about the art exhibit and they decided to go back to The Towers with us for the reception.

I could barely contain my excitement. Justine would be on hand to see me win my first blue ribbon ever. Except for the oyster, this had been a very good day.

Back at The Towers we all took elevators to the second floor and walked along a hallway to a room with a sign by the entrance that read GALLERY AT THE TOWERS. Justine was at my side, and as we waited near the doors

I said to her, "We had to *submit* our art ahead of time so it could be framed and hung and evaluated. Do you know what 'submit' means?"

Justine shook her head. "No. And I don't know what 'evaluated' means, either."

"'Evaluated' means 'judged,'" I told her importantly. "And 'submit' means . . ." I paused. I couldn't think of a good explanation. "Well, we had to send our pieces—our *art*—here ahead of time so the judges could look at everything and prepare the paintings for the show. There will probably be one first prize—that will be a blue ribbon—and one second prize—that will be a red ribbon—and then a lot of sad green consolation ribbons for all the losers."

Mrs. Means opened the doors to the gallery then, and Justine and I rushed inside. We were some of the first people in the room so I was able to spot my self-portrait right away. It hung in the center of the wall ahead of us.

"Justine, look!" I cried. "The blue ribbon is on my painting! I won! I won first place!" I tugged Justine through the gallery. "This is my very first self-portrait," I told her, "and the first painting I ever entered in a show. I can't believe I won!" Winning a blue ribbon in an art show was certainly something Lexie had never done.

We were about six feet away from my painting when I took a good look at the ribbon and saw the writing on it. It said GREAT ARTIST!

"Hey," said Justine then. "Everyone got first prize."

This was when I realized that a blue ribbon was stuck to absolutely every painting in the whole room, even crayon pictures by babies that were just like:

And they all said GREAT ARTIST!

"Where are the sad green ribbons?" Justine wanted to know.

Luckily Daddy Bo had followed us across the gallery, and he saved me from answering Justine. "Pearl, my gem of an artist," he said. "This is very impressive. A self-portrait! You certainly are talented."

"Yeah, especially compared to that," said Justine, pointing to one of the baby scribbles. And then she added, "You're the best artist I know, Pearl."

Which is one of the reasons Justine is still my old best friend, even if there are a lot of differences between us now.

"Thanks," I said.

We walked around the room and admired the paintings and nibbled at Fruit Roll-Ups and Cheez Doodles, which is what you do at an art exhibit. At four o'clock our parents started to arrive and I heard Mrs. Means say, "Don't forget to take your ribbons home with you."

That was when I got a good idea, and I snatched the ribbon off of my self-portrait and stuffed it in the pocket of my skirt.

IV. I rescued Bitey (cat).

I didn't stop talking once the entire time my father and I were riding the subway home. The doors closed behind us at 79th Street and I said, "I'll tell you about the whole day. First we had lunch, which was a buffet and you could eat whatever you wanted. Oh, and the server who scooped out the oysters for me? He said, 'Here you go, ma'am.' He called me ma'am!"

By the time the doors opened at 14th Street I was saying, ". . . and I won a blue ribbon. It's right here in my pocket." This was not a lie. I really had gotten a ribbon that was blue. I had just left out the part about all the babies getting blue ribbons, too.

A whole bunch of people streamed out behind us, and

I heard a lady say to another lady, "Do you think she stops to breathe?" which I certainly hope she wasn't talking about me because that's a rude thing for a grown-up to say.

I hopped along beside Dad on our way home and finally I said, "Did you have a good day?" and all he said was, "Yes," and sometimes you can just tell when a person doesn't feel like talking and is probably thinking about being fired and how the summer isn't really going the way he had planned.

When we got home, I found that Mom was working even though it was Saturday, so I bypassed her office and ran to Lexie's room and barged inside, completely forgetting the rule about knocking on closed doors.

"Guess what!" I cried. "Today was so much fun! We had a big buffet and I tried an oyster, and then I won *first prize* in the art show!"

I jammed my hand in my pocket, getting ready to pull the ribbon out. I planned to flash it in front of Lexie's face so fast that she wouldn't be able to see that it just lamely said GREAT ARTIST!

And that was when I realized my sister was crying.

She was lying on the bottom bunk with her face in the pillow, and frankly I don't know how she was able to breathe.

I wasn't sure what to do. I started to tiptoe out of the room, but Lexie hadn't yelled at me yet, and furthermore,

I could hear her sobbing in that awful adult way that's sort of loud and quiet at the same time.

I slid my hand back out of my pocket. Then I closed the door behind me and sat down on the edge of Lexie's bed. A year ago I wouldn't have been allowed to do this, but things had changed while we were roommates.

"Lexie?" I said quietly.

She sniffled and turned her head toward me. Her eyes were puffy, and her face was blotchy.

I almost said, "Are you okay?" but I knew what her answer would be: "What does it look like? Of course I'm not okay!" I thought of those newscasters who interview crying people after horrible disasters and ask them how they're feeling, and the crying people are always way too sad to reply, "Well, how do you *think* I'm feeling?" which is what you know they actually want to say.

"What happened?" I asked Lexie instead.

She sniffled again and drew in a shaky breath. "Dallas broke up with me."

My eyes widened. Lexie almost never gave me boyfriend information. I was trying to figure out what kind of advice I had on the subject when suddenly she leaped off the bed, reached for her cell phone, and held it out to me. "And you know *how* he broke up with me?" she went on. "He texted me. *Texted!* If you're going to do something like that to someone, you should at least have the nerve to tell the person to her face. Not just write, like, 'I think we should go out with other people,' which means he's *already* going out with someone else. I wonder who it is. It better not be Lindsey. If it's Lindsey, I'll—I'll—"

"Did you answer him?" I interrupted.

Lexie nodded furiously. "I sent him a text back five minutes ago, but I haven't heard anything yet."

I thought about Dallas, who I had liked because he had been nice to me even when Lexie was treating me like a baby. "Do you want *me* to send him a text?" I asked, even though I don't know how to do that since I don't have my own cell phone.

"No!" Lexie was on her feet instantly. "I mean, thank you. But definitely not. And don't call him, either," she added, eyeing me.

Lexie stayed in her room all evening, not even coming out for dinner on the family room floor, which was a sign of how upsetting it is to break up with your first boyfriend. The next morning my mother said to me, "Pearl, your dad and I are going to take Lexie to the Daily Grind. I think she needs a little treat. Can you stay at home by yourself for an hour?"

The breakup must have been very serious if Mom and Dad were going to spend $$ on coffee at the Daily Grind when they could make coffee at home for a lot less $$. And also if Mom and Dad were going to trust me alone

118

in the apartment when everyone knows how much trouble I can get into, even with adults around.

"Sure," I said.

"You won't be scared?" asked my father, just as my mother said, "And you'll stay put?" which she was probably remembering the time when Daddy Bo and I had left the apartment together and didn't tell anyone where we were going and accidentally went all the way to New Jersey and then there was a little trouble.

"I'll stay right here with Bitey," I said, glad that I wouldn't be entirely alone in the apartment. And wanting to prove how responsible I could be. Maybe when I turned eleven my parents would think back on my responsibleness and get me a cell phone.

Mom and Dad left a few minutes later with Lexie trailing sadly after them.

"Bye, Pearl," she said tragically to me as the apartment door closed. Her eyes were large and wet, even though she must have been thinking about ordering that whipped-cream coffee thing.

I wandered into the family room. I planned to see if there were any *I Love Lucy* reruns on TV, and if there were, to watch them with Bitey. He lies on my head and waves his tail back and forth in front of my face, which makes it a little hard to see the TV, but that's okay because I like his tail.

I looked around the living room. No Bitey.

"Where are you?" I said aloud.

I checked my bed and then Lexie's bunks and then Mom and Dad's big bed. No Bitey curled up on a pillow.

I looked under the beds. I looked behind the couch in the family room. I looked under Mom's desk. No Bitey.

"Bitey!" I shouted, even though he almost never comes when you call. "Bitey!"

A funny feeling crawled around in my stomach, a little bit of uneasiness. "Bitey?" I said.

I tried to think of all the strange places Bitey has chosen for naps—the shower in Mom and Dad's bathroom, the basket of onions on top of the refrigerator, Lexie's wastebasket. I looked in those places and didn't find him, and then I went from room to room and looked in every spot where Bitey could possibly fit and I still couldn't find him. I opened closets in case he had gotten locked in. I looked in the hallway in case he had escaped when Lexie and my parents had left. No Bitey anywhere at all.

I felt a lump forming in my throat. Mom and Dad had trusted me to stay by myself for the first time ever, and I had lost our cat. I tried to think how someone mature—Lexie, for instance—would handle the situation. She would call one of her friends on her cell phone, I decided. I was about to call JBIII on our regular non–cell phone when I noticed something that made me shiver. One of the family room windows was open. The safety guard was in place, but there's no screen behind it, and the bars of the guard are wide enough for a fat cat to squeeze through.

My heart began to pound so hard that I could feel it beating in my ears. I crossed the family room and peered out the window. Two floors below me was the terrace of apartment 5F, which belongs to the Olsons who are fun to spy on because in warm weather they eat breakfast outside in their pajamas and talk very loudly about television shows I'm not allowed to watch, and also sometimes Mrs. Olson goes out there and plays her flute, and let me tell you, even without one lesson I could play the flute better than she does.

Anyway, sitting on one of the Olsons' striped lounge chairs was Bitey. He didn't look hurt, but he looked embarrassed, the way I must have looked the time I decided to experiment with our blender, a jar of peanut butter, and a can of apricots, and realized too late why you're supposed to put the top on the blender.

"Bitey!" I called "Bitey!"

He turned his face toward me and mewed the tiny baby mew he uses when he's feeling especially pitiful about something.

"It's okay, Bitey!" I told him. "Don't panic. Stay right where you are."

I paused to think. Since Bitey wasn't hurt I knew I

could take time to do things the proper way and prove my responsibleness. One of the problems with the trip Daddy Bo and I had taken to New Jersey was that we hadn't told anyone where we were going. I realized I should probably call Mom on her cell phone now and tell her I was on my way to rescue Bitey, but I didn't really want to have a conversation with her about the open window, just in case she thought I was the one who had left it open, which I was not. So I found a pen and a pad of paper and I wrote:

Dear Mom and Dad and Lexie,
Back very soon. Rescuing Bitey, he's OK. Really.
Love, Pearl
P.S. I am safe. Really.

I left the pad on the floor of our foyer where no one could miss it. Next I closed the family room window. Then I found my key to the apartment, locked the door carefully behind me, and rode the elevator two flights down to the fifth floor. I knocked on the Olsons' door and waited. No answer. I knocked again, this time more loudly in case Mrs. Olson was in there hooting away on her flute. But when I pressed my ear to the door I didn't hear a sound. I knocked twice more and then, very slowly, I twisted the doorknob. My heart started to pound again. I knew I shouldn't go into an apartment uninvited, but this was an emergency. The knob wouldn't move, though. The door was locked.

I scurried back onto the elevator and rode it down to the lobby. Luckily, John was at the desk.

"John!" I cried. "John!"

John looked at me in alarm. "Pearl, is everything all right?"

I thought again about those newscasters, but I didn't want to be rude to John, so I just said, all breathless, "No! Bitey fell out the window. He isn't hurt. He landed on a chair on the Olsons' terrace. But I have to rescue him and the Olsons aren't home!" I paused. "And I was *not* the one who left the window open."

John was already on his cell phone, calling Etienne, who is the superintendent of our building, and you probably won't be surprised to learn that Etienne speaks with a French accent. The next thing I knew, Etienne and I were standing outside the Olsons' apartment and Etienne was jingling through the biggest ring of keys I'd ever seen.

"Ah-ha," he said at last. "Zees ees zee one." (That's really how he talks.) He opened the door, calling out, "Meester Olson? Meesiss Olson?" as he stepped inside. There was still no answer, so then Etienne said to me, "All right, Pell." (He has a very hard time with my name.) "Let us go."

Etienne led me through the apartment to a sliding-glass door. Beyond the door was the terrace with its deck chairs and potted plants and Mrs. Olson's flute case. I had expected to see Bitey waiting patiently for me, since I had told him to stay where he was and not panic. Instead, he had panicked completely and was jumping from chair to chair, looking for an escape. When he saw Etienne, he growled and leaped onto the terrace wall, which if he fell off of it, he would sail five stories down to the cement sidewalk of Twelfth Street.

"Bitey!" I shrieked, imagining what would happen if Mom and Dad and Lexie were on the way home right now and their cat suddenly shot out of the sky. I made a grab for Bitey and caught him around his middle. Then I hurried back inside the Olsons' apartment and Etienne closed the terrace door.

Bitey hissed and struggled in my arms, but I held on tight as we hurried through the living room. I was just thinking that I might be able to keep this entire adventure a secret from my family, when the Olsons' front door burst open and in rushed Mrs. Olson and Jasper. Jasper is a breed of dog that is extremely large, extremely loud, and extremely non-cute.

The next few seconds were kind of confusing. Clearly, Mrs. Olson had come in through the back door of the building and had not spoken with John, because she was completely surprised to find Etienne, Bitey, and me in her living room. She said, "Oh!" and tripped and fell over an umbrella stand, which I would have to remember to tell

JBIII about that. Jasper sprang up in the air in fear, and Bitey escaped from my arms and took a swipe at Jasper's nose when he landed. He missed, but Jasper yelped, and then Mrs. Olson said, "Get that thing out of here!" and I said, "I'm *try*ing," and Etienne said, "So sorry, Meesiss. Come, Pell."

Etienne took the regular elevator back downstairs while I rode to the seventh floor in the service elevator with Bitey. I half hoped Mrs. Mott would be on it for some reason and that Bitey would try to swipe at *her*, but it was empty, and before I knew it, Bitey and I were safely at home.

I was wondering again if there was any way at all that I could keep Bitey's accident a secret, when Mom and Dad and Lexie all came flying into our apartment and Mom said, "Is Bitey okay, Pearl?" and Dad said, "Poor old Bitey," and Lexie moaned and covered her face with her hands and said, "It's my fault. It's all my fault."

John had given them the news as they'd walked through the lobby. I couldn't really blame him for gossiping. It was one of the more exciting things that had happened in our building lately.

I was sitting on the couch in the family room with Bitey purring in my lap, and obviously we were both okay. Even so, I said uneasily, "Don't be mad." Then I added, "This wasn't my fault."

"I know! I know!" wailed Lexie. "It was *my* fault,

like I said. I opened the window. It's so hot today, and I was trying to save money by not using the air conditioner." My sister looked appealingly at our parents, and they didn't punish her due to the tragedy of breaking up with her boyfriend.

Mom and Dad sat down on the couch, one on either side of Bitey and me.

"I'm proud of you, Pearl," said Mom.

"Bitey is a lucky kitty," added Dad. "You knew just what to do."

"Did I act responsibly?" I wanted to know.

"Absolutely," said Mom.

"I think you deserve a reward," said Dad.

The reward turned out to be a lemonade at the Daily Grind and not a cell phone, but it was nice to sit in the air-conditioning with my parents all to myself and tell them the story of Bitey's adventure in great, great detail.

V. JBIII and I had a fight.

    A. It started at WaterWorks.

The next morning I woke up before anyone else in my family, including Bitey, who was still recovering from his unfortunate adventure. I knocked on my sister's closed door and let myself inside.

"It's already half over," I announced.

Lexie turned so that she was facing the wall. "What is?" she mumbled.

"Camp."

"So?"

"I just thought that was interesting."

"It isn't interesting at"—Lexie rolled over again and peered at the clock on her desk—"five twenty. Pearl, it's only *five twenty*! Nothing is interesting at five twenty in the morning. Go back to bed."

"Okay, but I'm not going back to sleep."

"Whatever."

I didn't see how my sister could possibly sleep. The last two weeks of camp were the best ones, I thought, as I lay on my bed, fully clothed and ready for the day. In three hours we would board the bus, and when we got to camp, the Starlettes and the Dudes and the other campers in my age group would have a big meeting with our counselors and some parent volunteers so that we could hear the list of reminders about Camp Merrimac rules and safety, blah, blah, blah, and *then* we would board the buses again and ride half an hour to Water-Works. In case you are one of the people, like JBIII, who has never been there, WaterWorks is New Jersey's premier outdoor water park. (That's what it says on their Web site. JBIII and I looked it up together on his parents' computer so he could have a chance to get excited about the trip beforehand.)

At WaterWorks there are about a million excellent water rides, three of which I'm too short for, that's how scary they are. You have to be either an adult or an abnormally tall child in order to qualify for the right to plummet through total darkness and get shot into a fake tide pool. But that's okay. There are plenty of other rides for shorter visitors.

"We *have* to go on River Rapids," I told JBIII. "That starts off as this nice, lazy raft ride along a river in Africa, if Africa were plastic, and then all of a sudden you're speeding through rapids, and at the very end an elephant sprays you with his trunk. Oh, and there's the Blizzard Blast, which is like a roller coaster through water."

"Why is it called Blizzard Blast?" JBIII wanted to know.

"Because before you get to the water, you're zooming around and around a mountain in the Yukon."

JBIII looked interested. "Huh," he said. "Is the water very cold?"

"No, just regular. But at the end of the ride is a stand where you can buy Blizzard Blast ice-cream cones." I looked at the Web site again. "Ooh, there's Thunder Alley. That's an excellent ride. So are the Jungle Swings and Island of the Lost. For little kids there's Pelican Beach and Toe Dippers and attractions like that, but we won't be interested in those."

I lay on my bed and thought about the water rides, and then I thought about the Garlic Festival, which the entire camp would be visiting at the end of the week, and then I thought about the last week of camp, which for the older kids—and that included JBIII and Lexie and me— was overnight camp, like in *The Parent Trap*. I got so excited thinking about all these things that by the time the Starlettes and the Dudes and the other ten- and eleven-year-olds were boarding the buses to WaterWorks later that morning, I sounded a little like Justine.

"JBIII!" I called as I ran down the aisle. "JBIII! Sit here with me!"

JBIII was already sitting next to a Dude, but I got hold of his arm and yanked him into an empty seat and plopped down next to him, completely ignoring the look that Lexie, who was one of the CITs on the trip, shot at me.

"Isn't this great?" I said. "I can't wait for River Rapids. I think we should go on that ride first. And then Thunder Alley. And after that we should eat lunch. Did I tell you that there are two places to eat? Well, two main places, and then there are ice-cream carts and cotton-candy carts and candy-apple carts all over the park, oh, and a store called Fine and Dandy, I Like Candy. Guess what it sells?"

"Candy?" asked JBIII.

"Yes, but more candy than you've ever seen in your life. There's a whole section of true penny candy. Each piece only costs one cent. Honest."

"I thought you didn't like candy."

"I don't like to *eat* it. But I like looking at it. You can buy candy necklaces and candy that crackles in your mouth—I might like to try that sometime—and chocolate that's shaped like New Jersey. Oh, oh—also there's a stand where you can buy personalized things like toothbrushes and key rings and little tiny license plates. They have every name you can think of. Except Pearl. I always mention that to the guy selling the stuff. I say, 'My name is Pearl. I don't see anything here with my name on it. You should alert somebody.' And he always says he will, but I've been to WaterWorks four times now with my family and I've never found anything personalized with 'Pearl.' Now that I think of it, 'JBIII' might be hard to find, too, but I bet you can find a lot of stuff that says James."

The buses were rolling along the highway by then. I paused to take a breath and felt in my pocket to be sure my money was there. It was, which was good, but I had less than half the amount I usually bring to WaterWorks. That morning Mom had given me enough money for lunch, and I had placed the bills carefully in my waterproof wallet along with the meager remains of my allowance. I would have to think very carefully about how to spend the money. There was the arcade with the games that spit out tickets for prizes, and the booth where you could get temporary body art. . . .

I wondered how much money Jill had brought. Fistfuls, probably. I imagined her getting on the bus in the afternoon carrying stuffed animals, her face painted like Cat Woman, and then she would sit with JBIII and she'd be all like, "*Hi*. Look what I won for you." And she'd give him a WaterWorks pen featuring a happy person sliding back and forth on a tiny raft.

I tried not to think about that and was in the middle of telling JBIII how we should spend our afternoon, when we turned into a sprawling parking lot, and ahead of us I saw the giant blue arch with WATERWORKS spelled out in dripping yellow letters.

"We're here," I said reverently. "This is it."

The bus drivers let us out near the entrance, and the very first thing that happened was that Edward, the drama counselor, who today was the counselor in charge of our trip, said, "Form groups of six, please." As fast as I could I grabbed JBIII, Juwanna, Deanna, and Misty, and then I let JBIII choose one Dude. I saw Jill edging toward us and I announced loudly to Edward, "We have six!" so then Jill tried to join the Bra Girls' group but it was full, too, and I don't know where she wound up. But Lexie wound up as my CIT, and Juwanna's mother and our counselor Janie wound up as the adults for our group.

At last our adventure could begin. We walked beneath the arch and through the Group Sales booth where we were each given a blue wristband that would let us onto all the rides.

Before us spread the wonderful world of WaterWorks.

"Now," I said to our group. "I've been here before." (Lexie eyed me sharply.) "I mean, my sister and I have been here before."

"Well, so have I," said the Dude, whose name was Cooper.

"Me, too," said one of the Starlettes.

I cleared my throat. "Anyway, we should go on River Rapids first. It's right over there. Come on, JBThree."

"Actually, if we want to split up, we can do that," said Janie, placing her hand on my shoulder. "There are two adults here, plus Lexie. Anybody want to start out on Thunder Alley?"

"I—" JBIII started to say.

But I was already walking toward River Rapids, hurrying JBIII along by the sleeve of his T-shirt. Cooper ran after us. We were followed by Lexie, Juwanna, and her mother. Ten minutes later I was whirling through the plastic African countryside, sitting behind JBIII, who kept shouting, "Whoa!" and then spluttering and laughing when we got sprayed with water.

"That was great!" he cried when the ride ended and

we met up with Juwanna's mother, who had been holding our stuff and taking pictures of us. "Let's go on it
again!"

"No," I said. "If we repeat rides we won't get to go on
all the good ones. Now, the next one should be Thunder
Alley."

"All right," said JBIII, who was eyeing the entrance to
Tunnel of Terror, where a bunch of Dudes in another
group were about to get hauled up four stories to the
top of a spooky enclosed water slide.

"Don't worry. We'll go on that one later," I assured
my best friend. "I planned the whole day, and that's an
afternoon ride."

JBIII frowned at me but said nothing.

After we'd gotten soaked on Thunder Alley we all
decided we were hungry, and I said, "The best place to
eat is Amazon Joe's."

"Pearl," Lexie said, and I knew she was going to re-
mind me that Amazon Joe's features mostly fried food,
and Mom and Dad would prefer that we eat the boring
salad-like food at Country Kitchen.

"Please?" I said to her. "We probably won't be back
here for another year."

Lexie smiled. "All right."

So we lined up at Amazon Joe's and I told JBIII the
best things to order and then we sat outside at little
round tables under grass jungle huts and ate our hot dogs

and French fries and onion rings. I still had enough $$ to order a vanilla milk shake for my beverage.

It was later, after Juwanna's mother had made us wait half an hour for our food to settle, that I noticed JBIII talking to Cooper. I edged closer to them and heard JBIII say, "Let's go on River Rapids again. That was an excellent ride."

"No!" I exclaimed, running to him. "You can't do that. It's time to—" I stopped talking when I saw JBIII's face.

He was frowning again, but it wasn't the kind of frown you make when you can't figure something out; it was the kind of frown you make when you've already swatted at a fly 65x and then you see it land on your arm again.

I changed the subject. "Look, there's the popcorn cart! Come on, let's buy popcorn!"

"Pearl, I don't want any popcorn," JBIII replied.

"But I do."

I realized just then that if I bought popcorn I wouldn't have enough $$ to buy a WaterWorks souvenir later. I was about to ask JBIII for a loan when he said quite loudly, "Unfortunately, you aren't the boss of me."

I took a step back. "I didn't say I was."

"Well, you've been acting like it all morning. You might as well put a leash on my neck and lead me around like a dog." (Cooper snorted at this, and even Lexie's face changed from surprise to amusement before she looked appropriately CIT-ish again.) "Maybe I don't want to do every single thing you want to do," JBIII went on. "Just leave me alone for a second, okay?"

I sat down on a bench for one second and then stood up again. "Was that long enough?" I asked. "Look. There's Tunnel of Terror. Let's go on that now."

"No! Pearl! Seriously. You're being a—" I don't know what JBIII was going to call me, but it couldn't have been anything very good because he suddenly stopped talking, and just in time—unlike the cabdriver I had annoyed on my birthday.

"Janie," he went on, "can Cooper and I please switch groups?" He looked wildly around WaterWorks and spotted a cluster of Dudes and Starlettes. "Randall!" he called. He held a quick conference with the Dude named Randall, and before I knew it, Randall and Mary Grace, the chattering Starlette, were switching places with JBIII and Cooper. And JBIII was getting strapped into an African river raft with three Dudes and a grinning Jill. JBIII was high-fiving Cooper and not paying any attention to Jill, but still.

"Well. What should we do now?" Juwanna's mother asked, and everyone automatically turned to me.

"I don't care," I said.

"Tunnel of Terror!" cried Mary Grace. "I already went on that twice, but I want to go again. It's so much fun.

Have you been on it yet? It's the coolest ride here. You have to try to sit in the very . . ."

Mary Grace would not stop gabbing and bossing. How could anyone stand her?

"Pearl?" said Lexie quietly. "Want to take a walk? We could try to find that stand with all the personalized stuff. Maybe they have your name now."

So Lexie and I got permission to walk around by ourselves for a while, and she gave me a dollar from her $$, which was very nice of her. But there were no Pearl things, and I was getting a stomachache from the onion rings and milk shake.

At three o'clock everyone met in the parking lot and lined up for the buses. I tried to talk to JBIII, but he pretended to be having such a thrilling conversation with Cooper that he didn't hear me. Then he waited until I had boarded the bus, and he walked down the aisle right past my seat and sat nine rows behind me, still jabbering away to Cooper.

He did the same thing an hour later when we were leaving Camp Merrimac to go home, except that he sat with this kid named Austin.

I sat with Justine, who was holding a wooden sailboat in her lap. She had made it that morning, and little pieces of it kept falling off as we drove along.

"Pearl?" she asked, as a paper sail loosened and came away from the mast. "Are you mad at me?"

"No," I said.

"Then why aren't you talking?"

Because I didn't feel like talking, that was why. I found a piece of paper in my backpack and wrote Justine a long note about my fight with JBIII. I passed it to her, and she stared at it and stared at it and finally was just like, "What?"

"Never mind."

The only good thing about the rest of the day was that I knew I could make up with my best friend in the morning as we walked to the bus.

V. JBIII and I had a fight.

  A. It started at WaterWorks.

  B. It continued at the Garlic Festival.

The next morning Lexie and I left our apartment and rode the elevator to the lobby. We sailed by John, who was engaged in a conversation with Mrs. Olson and was trying very hard to appear interested in what she called the blowhole on her flute, which I thought only whales had blowholes, but whatever.

I was thankful that Mrs. Olson didn't see me since I didn't want to have a conversation with her about Bitey's rude behavior. I ran outside and looked across the street, expecting to see JBIII in front of his building, but he wasn't there. Lexie and I waited for five minutes,

Lexie checking her watch approx. every eight to ten seconds, and finally she said, "Maybe he's sick today."

"Maybe," I said doubtfully.

"You want to ask his doorman to call his apartment?"

I squirmed. "Um, no."

Lexie stared at me. "Everything all right? Did you and JBThree make up yet?"

"Everything is totally fine."

"Okay. Well, let's go on to the bus stop. Maybe one of JBThree's parents will bring him later."

"Or maybe he's already there," I said hopefully.

He wasn't. And he still wasn't there when I caught sight of the bus chugging up Fourteenth Street. But a minute later when the bus was idling at the curb and we were starting to board, JBIII suddenly came hurrying along Sixth Avenue with his father.

I started to call to him, but Jill was standing in line behind me, and she pushed me up the steps, like she was in a great big hurry to be person #6 to get on at our stop. I sat in the first empty seat I saw and slid over to the window, leaving the aisle side free for my best friend. But JBIII walked past me, talking and laughing with Austin, and they found a seat in the back with a couple of other Dudes.

At least JBIII hadn't sat with Jill.

Lexie settled herself behind the bus driver, and I saw

her turn around and look at me like, "Is there anything I need to know?"

I shrugged and got a pad of paper out of my backpack and drew a picture of Jill encountering a water snake, even though none of this was really her fault.

Then I thought for a while and decided that JBIII was not the only one who could ignore people, and so I ignored him for the entire day at Camp Merrimac, including lunchtime and free time, and by the afternoon I thought he looked a little sad, like Bitey looks when he's found a Q-tip and you take it away from him before he can eat the cotton swab.

The buses arrived, and JBIII was the very first person to board ours. This time he sat by himself.

I walked past him.

Out of the corner of my eye I saw JBIII's mouth open and his brow crease into a frown, but this frown wasn't annoyed; it was sad and perplexed, like someone had given him a wonderful piece of candy that had mysteriously disappeared before he could put it in his mouth.

I sat down two rows behind JBIII, far enough to make my point, but near enough so that I could see him easily. JBIII kept turning around to look at me. The first time he looked, I pretended I was really interested in the back of Lexie's head. The second time he looked, I pretended to laugh hysterically at something Justine had said, even though she was, in fact, asleep. The third time, I glared at him for a moment, then casually got out my drawing pad and began sketching. JBIII whipped his head around to the front, the way Lexie and I whip our heads around when we're fighting and want to make the point that we aren't speaking to each other.

By the time the bus reached Fourteenth Street, I was mad and had drawn a comic strip about JBIII getting into a fistfight with a baby and losing. The last panel showed JBIII lying on the sidewalk on Twelfth Street with the baby standing on his chest and Mrs. Mott cheering for the baby.

I shoved my drawing pad into my backpack and followed Lexie off the bus. JBIII walked far in front of us all the way home. He didn't turn around once, but something about the way he was holding his head made me think he might be crying just a little.

Well, too bad.

That was Tuesday. On Wednesday, JBIII and I continued to ignore each other. We ignored each other on Thursday, too.

Friday was the Camp Merrimac trip to the Garlic Festival. Everyone in the whole camp was going: every camper in every age group, plus all the counselors and some parents. None of us had ever been to a garlic festival before, and to be honest, considering that I don't like garlic, the trip didn't sound like a whole lot of fun, even though Lisa had assured the Starlettes that despite the garlic theme, the festival was more like a county fair. I had a feeling it wasn't going to compare favorably to WaterWorks, but at least there would be some rides and arcade games.

By Friday, JBIII and I were not talking to each other just as much as we hadn't been talking to each other on Tuesday. I didn't feel hurt or mad anymore. What I felt was stubborn. And I wanted an apology from JBIII for making the leash/dog comment in public. I wouldn't have done that to him.

At 10:30 a.m. when Camp Merrimac descended on the Garlic Festival, I stepped off the bus with Justine.

"Let's be in the same group," I said to her.

"Really?" replied Justine, her eyes wide.

"Sure."

Justine and I joined a straggling bunch of kids who I think might have been eight- to nine-year-old Bumblebees, plus one six-year-old Apatosaurus. Whoever they were, JBIII wasn't among them, and neither was Jill or Cooper or Austin, and that was fine with me. I could have plenty of fun without any of them.

"Look!" cried Justine, pointing, as we walked through the entrance to the festival. "A giant—" She paused. "What is that? A giant egg?"

"I think it's a giant bulb of garlic."

"What *is* garlic anyway?"

"I'm not sure, but you wouldn't like it."

"How do you know?"

"I bit into some garlic once by accident. It made my eyes water just like the smell of our toilet cleaner does."

"Ew. Why would there even *be* a garlic festival?" asked Justine.

"I don't know. Adults must like garlic. But look— there's a Ferris wheel. That doesn't have anything to do with garlic."

"Oh! And baby animals! I see a barn full of baby animals."

The Garlic Festival wasn't so bad after all. It really was like a county fair, if you could ignore all the garlic. And since a ticket to the festival didn't cost nearly as much as a ticket to WaterWorks, Mom had given me more spending $$ than she had on Monday. I walked around with Justine and the Bumblebees and the Apatosaurus and we got our faces painted and rode the Ferris wheel and the bumper cars and finally a little train, which was slightly embarrassing because it was clearly for babies and was decorated with kittens playing with alphabet blocks, but whatever. Then we toured the animal barn, and since looking at the animals was free, Justine and I stayed in the barn for a long, long time.

"Do you think Mom and Dad would let me have a baby goat?" asked Justine. "Since I can't get my dog until I'm ten?"

I patted her on the arm and said probably not, and hoped she would forget about the goat by the end of the day.

Our group ate corndogs for lunch and I tried a drink called Ooh-la-la Orange, which turned out to be orange soda poured over a mound of ice chips. I was wiping an orange ring from around my mouth when I caught sight of JBIII and a bunch of Dudes sitting at a picnic table eating hamburgers and French fries. JBIII saw me, too, but then he just put another French fry in his mouth and turned to Cooper and was like, "Awesome bumper cars."

An hour or so later Justine and I had run out of $$, and the only thing left for us to do was look at stuff and try not to inhale the smell of garlic. Suddenly Justine grabbed my hand and said, "Hey! Clowns!"

Sure enough, two clowns were standing in front of a tent. One was selling helium balloons, and they were both posing for pictures. Little kids kept running to them and hugging them around their waists.

"You know what I've always wondered?" asked Justine. The rest of the kids in our group were riding the Tilt-A-Whirl, and we were sitting on a bench waiting for them. "I've always wondered about clown underwear. What do you think it looks like? Is it made especially for clowns? You know, like with ruffles and big polka dots? Or is it just regular underwear?"

I had never given any thought to clown underwear. "I don't know," I said.

"Let's go sneak in that tent. Maybe there are other clowns inside and we could see them changing into their costumes."

"No!" I cried. "I don't want to see naked clowns!"

"Well, maybe there's a rack of clown costumes we could look through. Come on, Pearl. Aren't you a little bit curious?"

I actually was. "Okay. But we'll just *peek* through that tent flap," I said, pointing, "and if anyone is naked in there, we'll turn around and run. Promise me, okay?"

"Pinkie swear," said Justine, extending her hand, so I knew she was serious.

We tiptoed around to the side of the tent, out of sight of the clowns posing for pictures. I looked over my shoulder to make sure no one was watching us, and then I snaked my hand through the tent flap.

"Close your eyes!" I whispered to Justine.

We squeezed our eyes shut, and I pulled the flap aside.

"Okay, now open them."

We blinked our eyes back open and squinted into the dim light. I could see a man sitting on a metal folding chair, reading a newspaper. He was wearing blue jeans and a T-shirt. There were some other things in the tent—a table and some packing cartons, several tanks of helium for blowing up the balloons—but no naked clowns, no clothed clowns, and no clown costumes.

"Rip-off," muttered Justine in disgust. She stepped backward, and I let the flap fall closed.

"Oh, well," I said.

I turned to look at the Tilt-A-Whirl. A new group of people were clambering onto the ride.

"Where are the Bumblebees?" asked Justine.

I glanced at the bench where we had been sitting. It was empty. I looked at the Tilt-A-Whirl exit. No Bumblebees. No Apatosaurus. I looked at a hot-dog stand and the animal barn and the entrance to the midway. I didn't see a single familiar person.

"Um, I don't exactly see them," I said.

"You mean we're lost?!" cried Justine.

Technically, we weren't lost, since I knew we were at the Garlic Festival.

"Now, don't panic," I said, remembering last Halloween when Justine and I had accidentally gotten locked in the basement of our apartment building and Justine had screamed and cried and shrieked before she got distracted by her bucket of candy long enough for me to save us.

"But where *is* everyone?" Justine wailed.

"I don't know." I had to admit that it was a little scary to look around and around and not see one face I recognized and also not be able to call for help on a cell phone, which, by the way, I had seen two kids younger than me at the Garlic Festival talking away on what were clearly their own personal cell phones.

I was tempted to panic, too, but luckily I remembered the incident at the Museum of Natural History and caught myself before I yelled, "Help! Police!"

I drew in a long, deep breath and let it out again. "Okay, here's—"

"HEEEEELP!" yelled Justine.

I clapped my hand over her mouth and left it there while I scanned the crowd for a police officer. I didn't see one, but I did see a tent with a red cross and the words FIRST AID and LOST AND FOUND by the entrance.

"Justine," I said, my hand still over her mouth, "see that tent? That's where we go to get help."

I led Justine to the tent and found an official-looking woman sitting at a small table. She glanced up at us and smiled. "Can I help you?"

"Yes," I replied in my most pleasant, calm voice. "I found this little girl here and I think she's lost."

This was not hard to believe, since Justine was sniffling, and tears were running down her dusty cheeks, leaving grimy trails that made her look like a movie orphan.

"All righty," said the woman. She turned to Justine. "And what is your name?"

"Justine Lebarro."

The woman turned back to me. "Where did you find her?"

I pointed to the clown tent. "Right over there."

"We were spying on the clowns and we lost the Bumblebees," said Justine.

The woman looked puzzled. At last she said, "Are you together? Are you both lost?"

Justine nodded and two more tears escaped from her eyeballs. "Yes. We are both lost. I am Justine Lebarro and she is Pearl Littlefield and we have to find our counselors from Camp Merrimac."

"All righty," the woman said again. She reached for a microphone, and my heart began to pound.

"Wait!" I cried.

But it was too late. "Attention! Attention!" said the woman. "I have two lost little girls here at the Information Tent. Their names are Justine Lebarro and Pearl Littlefield. They're looking for their camp counselors. Please come to the Information Tent. Repeat I have two lost little girls—Justine Lebarro and Pearl Littlefield." Her voice blared across the grounds of the Garlic Festival.

The good thing was that in less than five minutes Lisa and Lexie came running into the tent. The bad thing took place approx. twenty minutes later when we had boarded the buses and were on our way back to camp.

I took a seat by the window next to Eliza, the crying Starlette, and many rows away from Justine. I hoped no one would notice me. But the bus hadn't even left the parking lot when I heard a familiar voice call, "Help! Police!"

In front of me I saw the Bra Girls start to laugh.

Jill called out, "Help! Police!" again more loudly and added, "I'm a lost little girl."

Juwanna, Mary Grace, Misty, Austin, and Cooper started to laugh, too.

I craned my neck around in search of JBIII and spotted him in the back of the bus. He wasn't laughing. But he wasn't exactly not laughing, either, if you must know.

I swiveled around and stared out the window.

V. JBIII and I had a fight.

    A. It started at WaterWorks.

    B. It continued at the Garlic Festival.

    C. I almost made up with JBIII, but then I didn't.

On Monday morning I stood in our front hall and looked at the mound of stuff piled there: two sleeping bags, two jam-packed duffel bags, two backpacks, and a shopping bag full of things I hoped to be able to bring with me to Camp Merrimac, but was pretty sure my parents would ask me to leave at home. Really, though, how was I supposed to spend five days and four nights at overnight camp without my postcard collection, my first-prize ribbon from the art show, my miniature Statue of Liberty, my calendar for crossing off the days, my scrapbook, my stuffed dolphin, and the pillow that Lexie had made for me when she learned how to sew?

"What's all this?" asked Dad when he saw the bag.

I stepped in front of it. "Nothing."

Dad leaned over my shoulder and peered down into the bag. "Everyone is allowed one duffel bag and one backpack," he said. "That's it. No extras. There isn't much room in the cabins. Besides, your things will be safer if you leave them here. What if they get lost at camp?"

I squirmed. I'd never been away from home before, not without at least one member of my family along with me. Well, I had been to sleepovers at Justine's, but that was when Justine lived down the hall from us and I could run back to our apartment, if necessary.

Mom came into the hall then with a list in her hand. It was a list of all the things each overnight camper was supposed to pack for a week of sleepaway camp, and it was very specific, like: 5 prs. socks, 5 prs. underwear, 3 prs. jeans, 3 prs. shorts, 5 shirts, 1 pr. pajamas, one towel, one washcloth, bathing suits, cap with brim, sunblock, etc., etc., etc.

Lexie had insisted on doing her own packing, and Mom had insisted on packing for me, and each of them had followed the list so carefully you would have thought it was actually a list of instructions for how to never get burned up in a fire. I had spied on Lexie through her partially open door while she was following the list and had heard her counting clothing as she pulled things from her drawers: "Socks, one, two, three, four, five. Underwear, one, two, three, four, five. Jeans, one, two, three." Mom had done the same thing when she was packing for me. Each of them had just barely managed to get everything crammed into one duffel bag and one backpack. That was why I had to pack my extra shopping bag.

Now I looked at Mom holding the list in our hallway. "You aren't going to re-check that, are you?" I asked. She had already re-checked the list once, the night before, ticking off the items in my duffel bag and backpack.

"No, I suppose not," she said uncertainly.

My father looked meaningfully at the shopping bag. "Pearl?" he said.

I carried it back to my room and left it sitting in the middle of the floor where Mom and Dad would see it while I was gone and realize how sad it must have made me to be separated from my favorite possessions the first time I was away from home by myself.

"All right!" called Dad. "Time to get a move on!"

Lexie and I had so much gear to lug to camp that both Mom and Dad walked with us to Fourteenth Street. When the bus arrived the driver helped us stow our things and then Mom and Dad hugged Lexie and me forever and Mom was all, "Remember to put your sunblock on every morning. And eat a good big breakfast. And don't stay up late. And remember to brush your teeth. And listen to your counselors. And try to set aside a little time for reading. And Pearl, please change your underwear every single day." And Dad was just like, "Have fun!" and then he gave us the sad smile I'd been seeing ever since he became a fired person.

All of this was only a little embarrassing, because Jill's parents and JBIII's parents and Austin's parents were doing the same things, except not smiling sadly, since none of them had been fired.

I sat by myself on the way uptown and ignored the occasional calls of "Help! Police!" After the 79th Street stop I sat with Justine. She looked alarmed by the mound of duffel bags and sleeping bags in the back of the bus and said she was never, ever going to sleep away from her parents, even when she was a grown-up.

I began to feel a little nervous about overnight camp. What if I got a stomachache in the middle of the night? What if I didn't like the camp food? After all, I didn't like the birdseed snacks. What if I couldn't fall asleep in the cabin? *What if I had to share a cabin with Jill?*

I felt a little better after we arrived at Camp Merrimac, though. Lisa told us there were two cabins for the Starlettes, and then she read off who would be where, etc., etc., etc., and I was in Sunrise Cabin and Jill was in Blue Jay Cabin, so that was one worry out of my mind.

(FYI, the other girls in my cabin were Juwanna, Misty, Deanna, Mary Grace, and Denise.)

All the kids in the ten- to eleven-year-old groups and the twelve- to fourteen-year-old groups spent the morning getting settled in their cabins and then going to a meeting about what it means to be a Merrimac overnight camper. (In case you're wondering, a Merrimac overnight camper is polite, responsible, respectful, and follows the rules. I have to admit that that didn't quite sound like me, but whatever.) We also found out that we would get to have some cookouts and campfires and go to a movie in the recreation hall. The especially good thing about these activities was that they were free.

During the meeting I looked at Lexie, who was taking notes, since she would be the Starlettes' CIT on Tuesday and Thursday evenings in addition to the afternoons, and she didn't want to make any mistakes. Then I looked at JBIII, who was sitting with the Dudes and punching Austin on the arm, and I thought how much more fun the week would be if my best friend and I were speaking to each other.

But we were not.

By 5:00 in the afternoon all the younger campers had gotten on their buses and gone home. The rest of us had free time until our first Camp Merrimac supper. Lexie was busy with her friends far away in Juniper Cabin, and the Starlettes were sitting outside talking in whispers, but not about me. I was sitting on my bunk in Sunrise Cabin, looking around. This is what is in a Camp Merrimac cabin: three wooden bunk beds built into the wooden walls; a single wooden bed for our cabin counselor, who was Janie; one wooden shelf over each wooden bed. That's it. No chairs, no tables, and did you notice that I didn't mention lamps? That's because there's no electricity in the cabins. Now I understood why "flashlight" had been included on the packing list.

Did you also notice that I didn't mention anything about bathrooms? That is correct. There are no bathrooms in the Camp Merrimac cabins. The only bathrooms at camp are the ones next to the director's office, the two (wooden) buildings named Goose Lodge and Gander Lodge (which I had to explain those names to Justine the first time she went to Camp Merrimac). Goose Lodge and Gander Lodge are fine during the day when we can run to them at any moment and see where we're going in the bright sunlight. But as I sat on my bunk on Monday afternoon I wondered what would happen if I had to go to the bathroom in the middle of the night. I tried to imagine climbing down off of the top bunk without waking anyone up, turning on my flashlight, and then walking through the woods in the pitch-dark wearing only my pajamas. I had no idea what kinds of animals are in the woods in New Jersey after dark, but I imagined that a lone girl in her nightie might be a target for them, whatever they were.

I wanted to discuss this with JBIII, but as you know, my best friend wasn't talking to me.

I found a piece of paper and started a letter to my parents:

Dear Mother and Father,
This is your daughter, Pearl Littlefield. I am at camp and we have a bathroom situation. Which is that the bathrooms are not in the cabins—they are about ten miles away. And I don't think you want me walking through the woods alone at night, do you?

I paused. I realized that even if I could mail the letter to my parents that very second, they probably wouldn't receive it until Wednesday or Thursday, which would be too late, bathroom-wise.

I had just realized that the whispering outside had become laughing and yelling when someone came crashing through the door to our cabin. "Pearl!" It was Juwanna. "Pearl, come on! We're going to have a water fight. Sunrise against Blue Jay. We need you. Here are some balloons. Go fill them with water."

I slid down off my bunk. I happen to be an expert with water balloons. In fact, we've had a little trouble at

157

home on the occasions when I've dropped them out our windows. Once, one landed on Mrs. Olson's head while she was standing on her patio admiring the view of Twelfth Street. But if my parents could have seen me now they would have realized that my practice was paying off.

Juwanna and Mary Grace and I hid behind Sunrise Cabin and when Bra Girls #1 and #2 sneaked over from Blue Jay we ambushed them with the balloons. Eventually we won the whole fight on account of insects. I yelled at Vonna to watch out for the ants' nest (which there wasn't one) and she screamed and fell down and all the Blue Jay girls ran to her and Juwanna and I threw the rest of our balloons at the Blue Jay Cabin and when one went through a window and exploded on Jill's bed we declared ourselves the winners.

The Starlettes arrived at the mess hall, which is camp talk for cafeteria, dripping wet and we ate our suppers dripping wet, too, and no one said anything about that so I officially decided that overnight camp was all right even though I hadn't had to go to Goose Lodge by myself in the dark yet.

Guess what. I never did go to Goose Lodge by myself in the dark. I collapsed onto my bed that night before nine o'clock and fell asleep instantly and didn't wake up until there was sunlight shining through the windows of the cabin. I slept like that every night I was at Camp

Merrimac, which was good because then I could honestly tell my mother that I hadn't stayed up late. In fact, I was so tired from Camp Merrimac activities that when I woke up after my first night it was only because Juwanna had climbed onto my bunk and was shaking my shoulder and saying, "Pearl! Get up! You slept through the morning horn."

"What morning horn?" I mumbled. I tried to open my eyes.

"That big loud horn that was blaring in our ears for five minutes. I can't believe you didn't hear it." She shook me again. "Come *on*. You have to get up and get dressed right this second. We're supposed to be at the mess hall and we can't be late."

"But I'm not ready to get up." I rolled over and closed my eyes.

Then I heard another voice from below. It was Janie's voice and it was saying, "No time to get dressed now, Pearl. You'll have to go to breakfast in your pajamas." When she added, "And I mean it," I got up, put on my sneakers, and followed the rest of the Starlettes through the woods to the mess hall. I noticed that I wasn't the only camper still in my pajamas. I wasn't even the only Starlette still in my pajamas.

The first thing I saw when I entered the mess hall was a giant bowl of birdseed at the end of a table full of food. But beyond the birdseed was regular stuff like corn flakes and scrambled eggs and bread and yogurt (which I personally think tastes like milk mixed with barf, but at least it's normal food) and melon and orange juice.

I fixed myself a plate of eggs and toast and sat with Juwanna and with the two other Starlettes who were wearing their pajamas. There was sunshine streaming through the windows of the mess hall and everyone was laughing and talking and I didn't think I was homesick, and suddenly I felt so happy that I decided to keep a diary of the rest of my week as an overnight camper.

<u>Tuesday</u>
Day started when slept thru morning horn and had to go to breakfast in pajamas. Embarrassing but fun.

Note: Did NOT have to go to Goose Lodge in middle of night. I think there are bears here even tho Janie says there are not.

Saw Justine at lunchtime. Said she sat with Apatosaurus on bus in morning. Seemed a little bite mad at me.

After supper which was cookout with hot dogs, Starlettes decided to put on show for Janie and Lisa.

Since we had already had a talent show we decided to put on a play, and I said, "I think we should put on *The*

Wizard of Oz and Jill should be Dorothy. Or maybe Glinda, that beautiful witch."

I saw Juwanna give me a strange look, but Jill was like, "Wow, you think I'm pretty?"

And I was like, "Yeah. You could be a model."

And the result of all this was that we put on a good play, even though we didn't have costumes, and also Jill never said "Help! Police!" in front of me again.

After show, we all went to bed even though only 8:49 p.m. Looked out window by bunk. Are more stars in New Jersey than New York. Also, night is darker, as black as inside of closet when light is turned off. Really hope do not have to go to Goose Lodge alone tonight.

Wednesday

So far have not lost any cloths. Found packing list in duffel bag and checked all clothing and other items and everything is here. Do not miss postcard collection.

Also, did not have to go to Goose Lodge last night.

Also, did not have to go to breakfast in pj's.

BEST thing happened after lunch. Hit HOME RUN!!! Finally!!!

By the softball field was a big board with a chart listing every camper's name, and next to the names were spaces where the counselors made a red X each time one of us hit a home run. Lexie had hit a few home runs during the summer, and so had JBIII, even though he isn't especially sporty, and, well, everyone had hit at least one, except for me and two of the Apatosauruses. After lunch on Wednesday the Starlettes decided to have a game of softball, Sunrise Cabin against Blue Jay Cabin, and Bra Girl #2 was pitching to me and there was silence since cheering for me was pointless but booing was a little rude, and the next thing I knew I heard a *crack!* and the ball was sailing through the air.

"Run! Run, Pearl!" Juwanna yelled.

So I started running and I made it to first base and I heard voices shouting, "Keep going!" so I did, and I rounded second and everyone was shouting, "Go! Go!" so I kept going, and the next thing I knew I was back at home plate, and way off in the outfield I saw Lena finally find the ball.

"You did it!" I heard another voice shout, and I looked up and there was Lexie. "You did it, Pearl!" She was grinning, and she handed me a red marker. "You should make your own X."

Lexie took a picture of me marking my first Camp Merrimac home run X on the chart, and later I put the

photo in my scrapbook along with all my other camp
mementos.

Thursday

Did not have to go to Goose Lodge in pitch
dark last night.

Woke up early this morning, before blaring horn,
looked out window and saw TWO DEER outside
cabin. One was mother and one was spotted
baby that was leaping around like Bitey.

Excellent thing happened before dinner, not as
good as home run X but still pretty good. Won
ping-pong turniment in 10–11 age group and when
Lisa gave me button that said CHAMPION saw
JBIII smiling at me from Dude group. Thought
about making up with him, but time was not right,
what with Dudes around.

Tomorrow will apologize privately to best friend
for bossy behavior.

VI. There was an accident.

Friday was my last day at Camp Merrimac. I woke up early and first I realized that I'd made it through the whole week without having to go to Goose Lodge in the middle of the night, and then I looked out the window and saw the mother deer and her little baby again. (FYI, all this was taking place *before* the morning horn, so note that I was being a responsible, non-tardy Merrimac overnight camper.) The mother and I watched each other for a while and finally I said to her, "You have a very nice baby," and she stiffened her legs and then ran away with her eye whites showing as if I had actually said, "I plan to steal your baby and raise him in New York City."

From across the cabin Juwanna said, "Who are you talking to, Pearl?"

"No one," I replied, and I got dressed quickly so as not to have to go to breakfast in my pajamas.

Even though I liked sitting with the Sunrise Starlettes and eating Camp Merrimac breakfasts (except for the birdseed and milk-barf), I decided to eat by myself on Friday morning. I wanted to think about JBIII and when I should talk to him, and what I should say to him when I apologized. The timing would be a little tricky since this was Visiting Day, and the families of all the Merrimac campers would start to arrive well before lunch, so I didn't really have much time.

I took a bite of a muffin and chewed and thought about my best friend and how our fight had begun and what I could do to end it. I decided I would find JBIII in a quiet moment after breakfast. I would say to him, "JB-Three, can we please talk for a minute?" But I would say this in a polite manner, not like a principal who would say it so sternly that you would know that what the principal actually meant was, "You are in deep trouble and we need to have a meeting right now in my official office and then I may have to phone the police and have you arrested."

JBIII would say, "Yes, of course, Pearl," also in a polite manner, not a sarcastic one, and then I would say—

I thought some more. What *would* I say? It's a little hard admitting that you were bossy and were giving orders and making your friend feel like a dog on a leash. And also that your best friend had wanted you to go away and leave him alone. Especially when what *you* had wanted was for your best friend to get the most out of his first trip to WaterWorks. But I could sort of see how my orders might have been taken the wrong way.

So how I would apologize to JBIII was like this: "I've been thinking about our fight and I want to tell you that I'm very sorry we had it." Then I would take a big breath and get really truthful. "I was being bossy and that wasn't nice. I wanted you to have a good time at WaterWorks and instead I ruined everything." I wondered whether, if I started to cry, my apology would be more believable, or if JBIII would just get embarrassed by girl tears and run away.

I gave up the idea. I didn't want JBIII to run away and I definitely didn't want him to accept my apology just because he felt sorry for me.

After breakfast all of us overnight campers had to return to our cabins and pack up our stuff, except for the things we would need during the day. So we did. This took a while and when I finished I realized that our families would be arriving soon. If I was going to apologize to JBIII, now was the time.

I stepped out of Sunrise and looked around, and what

was the first thing I saw but JBIII in his bathing suit heading for the lake. He had a good head start, so I began to run after him, and I ran all the way to the lake and had just about caught up with him when he stepped onto the dock. I kept running. I ran right by the rules sign on the back of the lifeguard stand and I called, "James Brubaker the Third!"

JBIII turned around and I kept running and FYI, it turns out there's a good reason the very first rule on the sign is NO RUNNING ON THE DOCKS. A lot of lake water had sloshed over the wooden boards and made them slippery, and believe you me it is scary to suddenly find that your legs are sliding out from under you and you have no control over them.

I crashed feet-first into JBIII, and even before I landed I watched my best friend hurtle backward and smash into an upturned canoe resting on the end of the dock.

"OW!" I cried as I sat down hard on my bottom, but JBIII didn't make any sound, which is scarier than you can imagine.

I sat up, and a little part of me was wondering if I had splinters in my bottom and how big my bruise was going to be, and thinking that a bruised, splintery bottom would be embarrassing. But the rest of me was concentrating on JBIII, who sat slumped silently against the canoe. His eyes were open, but he still hadn't said a word. He hadn't even moaned.

I forgot about my bottom.

"JBIII?" I said.

No answer.

"*JBIII?*"

"I'm hurt," he finally whispered, and I noticed that his arm was hanging at a strange angle.

I jumped to my feet and leaned over JBIII. I tried to think how Lexie would handle a first-aid emergency like this one. When Lena had gotten hurt playing softball Lexie had sent someone for the nurse and an ice pack and the stretcher. And then she had stayed with Lena until help came. She had not touched Lena's leg.

I said very calmly, "It's going to be okay, JBIII," and I didn't touch his arm. I straightened up and was about to scream for the lifeguard when I realized that the lifeguard had seen the whole accident and was already running along the dock.

"Don't run!" I shouted at him.

The lifeguard, a counselor named Doug, didn't pay any attention to me. He knelt by JBIII, spoke to him for a moment, and then started shouting into a walkie-talkie spy thing that I hadn't noticed he was holding. He gave a whole lot of orders and finally said, "I think he broke his elbow."

After that there was a lot of confusion. The nurse, the camp director, a bunch of counselors including Lexie, and an even bigger bunch of campers all came running down the dock, completely ignoring the rules sign. Everyone crowded around JBIII, and Lexie shouted, "Stand back!" while Doug tried to help JBIII to a more comfortable spot, but JBIII said he was going to faint, and refused to move.

I edged to the front of the crowd. "Does it hurt a lot?" I asked my best friend (who hadn't fainted).

"Yes," he whispered. I noticed that he didn't look at me, but this might have been because of the pain, etc., etc., etc.

There was a scuffle at the end of the dock, and two counselors came pushing through the crowd with the stretcher. They were just sliding JBIII onto it when I saw another herd of people arrive at the lake and I realized that this was a herd of families and visitors. At the head of the herd were Mr. and Mrs. Brubaker, JBIII's parents.

Mrs. Brubaker knelt down beside JBIII and he began to cry, and then so did I, since I had sort of caused all the trouble.

Mr. Brubaker turned to the camp director. "How long will it take the ambulance to get here?"

The ambulance? My stomach turned to ice water.

"About twenty minutes, I'd say," was the reply.

"We can get him to the hospital faster ourselves," said Mr. Brubaker.

And the next thing I knew the entire herd of people had hurried back to the camp entrance and JBIII's parents were settling him in their car.

I heard a voice call to the Brubakers, "You go on! Don't worry, we'll bring his things home for you!" I realized the voice belonged to my father. He and Mom and about a billion other parents along with brothers and sisters and aunts and uncles had now arrived. All at the same moment, Dad turned to me and said, "You can help us gather up JB's things, can't you?" and Mom said, "Pearl, do you know how the accident happened?" and Lexie said, "I just hope he won't need surgery."

Then from behind me I heard one more voice: "Poor, poor Jamie." I turned around. Jill was standing there holding her Camp Merrimac baseball cap over her heart, and her voice was trembling in the fake way that mine does when I try to make myself cry in order to convince Mom and Dad that their parenting tactics are unfair.

I didn't answer either my mother or my father. I walked away from my family, and I kept walking until I had reached Sunrise Cabin. I lay down on one of the bare wooden bunks and stared across the room.

I had broken my best friend's elbow. My best friend already thought I was bossy and mean, and hadn't spoken to me in nearly two weeks. And he didn't know that I wanted to apologize to him. What he did know was that I broke rules and had ruined the rest of his summer, and now no one would get to hear him recite his Write Right story, which he had won a Merrimac award for it.

Two tears leaked out of my eyes and ran down into my hair.

"Pearl?" It was my mother.

"Go away." I turned to face the wall.

"Don't worry about JB, honey," she said. She stepped into the cabin, sat beside me, and began to pat my back. "He broke his elbow but he's going to be fine. Bones heal."

"You don't understand," I said. "I *made* him break his elbow. I was running on the dock, which is against the rules, and I slipped and bumped into him and he fell down. And that's how he broke his elbow."

"Oh, dear," said my mother. "I see why you're upset. But, Pearl, that was an accident. You didn't do it on purpose."

I put my hands over my face. "I wasn't supposed to be running on the dock." I didn't add that lately I had been an absolutely horrible friend to JBIII.

"I understand that. But it was still an accident. When JB is feeling better you can apologize to him, all right? I'll talk to his parents later. And the next time you're on one of the docks you'll remember the rules. Would you feel better if you could do something for JB?"

I uncovered my face. "I guess so."

"Then show me to his cabin and you can help me

with his things. We'll drive them back to the city this afternoon and leave them at his building."

"Did you borrow Mrs. Mott's car again?" I asked.

My mother sighed. "Yes. So we'll have to be very careful when we load it up. Also, you and Lexie should each write her a thank-you note for allowing us to use the car."

I didn't say anything.

"Pearl?"

"Okay."

My mother and I made our way to the Dude cabins, which inside and out looked exactly like the Starlette cabins, and we found JBIII's bunk, with his sleeping bag and duffel and backpack sitting neatly on it in a row. I picked up the sleeping bag and Mom picked up the duffel and backpack and we carried them across Camp Merrimac to Mrs. Mott's car and stowed them in the trunk.

"Can we go home now?" I asked.

"What? But it isn't even lunchtime," my mother replied. "We'll miss all the activities. The cookout and the display of your work and the show you're going to put on."

"I don't feel like doing any of that."

My mother looked as if she didn't feel so sorry for me anymore. "Lexie might feel like it, though," she pointed out.

I let out a sigh, this one much bigger and louder than my mother's, and followed Mom through the parking lot and back to the field where the Merrimac campers, all of them, were singing the songs we'd learned during the past month. My mother gave me a little shove toward the performers, but I didn't feel like joining them. I dropped down onto a wooden bench next to my father and in front of Justine's parents and sat there with my arms folded across my chest.

I saw my father glance at my mother, then at me, and raise his eyebrows, and I heard my mother whisper, "I'll tell you later."

I wondered about JBIII and what was happening to him at that very moment. Was he crying again? Was the doctor putting a cast on his arm? Would JBIII have to spend the night in the hospital?

I could feel tears in my eyes and I swiped at them. My mother tried to stroke my hair then and I pushed her hand away and my father said in his warning voice, "Pearl," so I flumped off and turned my back on the rest of the performance.

When the show was over it was time for the cookout. I sat by myself at a table with a hot dog that I didn't want, and watched Lexie walk around and around with her arm linked through a boy's arm. I knew who he was. Liam, the Apatosauruses' morning CIT. Once, when Lexie and Liam orbited by my table, I heard my sister say, "Lexie and Liam. Even our names go together! It's, like, fate."

So I guessed that my sister had gotten over Dallas. But I knew for a fact that Liam lived in New Jersey, not in New York City, and I wondered how he and Lexie would get to spend any time together and if, when Lexie began to miss him, she would moon around our apartment and put up the NO PEARL sign and play sad melodies on her violin.

When camp was finally over my parents and my sister and I got into Mrs. Mott's car and drove home. We dropped off JBIII's things at his apartment building, and then we returned the car to the garage, and my parents felt so sorry for me that they bought me a gumball from the machine. Later, I sat in my bedroom with the door closed and chewed and decided that I had probably lost my best friend—and he had only been my best friend for a few months. It hadn't taken me long to ruin everything.

At dinnertime my mother said, "Pearl, I think it would be nice if you called the Brubakers to find out how JB is doing."

"You call," I said.

My mother gave me a look and handed me the phone. I shook my head. "I just can't."

So Mom called and it turned out that JBIII was already at home and he was going to be fine. "Pearl feels terrible," I heard my mother say a few moments later, and then, "Well, thank you for understanding. . . . Yes . . . Okay. I'll check in tomorrow."

I was glad that JBIII was going to be fine, but it didn't change what I had done to him.

After supper I tried to write a note to JBIII, but I couldn't. I scrunched up twenty-four pieces of notebook paper before I realized that there was no good way to apologize to your friend for nearly killing him. So then I just wrote the thank-you to Mrs. Mott.

> Dear Mrs. Mott,
> Thank you for lending us your clean car so Mom and Dad could drive to camp for visiting day. It was a wonderful day, which wouldn't have been so wonderful if Mom and Dad couldn't have driven there. So I'm very greatful for your generosity and for all the storage space for our sleeping bags and duffles. You are a very kind neighbor. Please let me know if there's ever anything I can do for you.
> Your friend,
> Pearl Littlefield

I didn't mean the last part of the letter at all and hoped Mrs. Mott wouldn't take me up on my offer. I left the insincere note on my mother's desk and went to bed without saying good night to anyone.

VII. My family went on a lame staycation.

   A. We pretended to be tourists in our own city.

Remember the staycation my parents mentioned? Well, they were still planning it. In fact, they were very excited about it. Almost every day for the past month, Lexie and I had found another flyer or newspaper article or photo of the Brooklyn Bridge lying on the kitchen counter to get us excited.

SKYSCRAPER!

See Three Major Attractions for One Low Price!

PLAN YOUR VISIT NOW!

Wonder of the Age: Master Painters (that was an article about an exhibit at the Metropolitan Museum of Art)

Meet the Tree Toad (that might have been for something at the Museum of Natural History, which I hoped we wouldn't have to go there)

Mom and Dad sure wanted to keep Lexie and me entertained on our Wild West–free summer. The staycation was to begin the day after camp ended.

True to their word, Mom and Dad were taking vacation for nine whole days—a weekend, a week, and the weekend after that. No writing for Mom and no job hunting for Dad. I tried to find some enthusiasm for the staycation, but two things were wrong:

1. I couldn't stop thinking about JBIII. Less than twenty-four hours had passed since I had broken his elbow and also not apologized for any of the things I had done to him so far this summer.

2. I'm sorry, but I still *really* wanted to go out west. At the very least, I wanted to see a ghost town. A tree-toad exhibit just didn't measure up to cowboys and panning for gold and graveyards with moonlit tombstones.

But . . .

"We can be tourists in our own city!" said Mom on Saturday, the day after camp ended. "We'll do all the things here that we never seem to have time for."

"What are we going to do today?" I asked. I tried to smile.

"We were thinking of starting off slowly, maybe just having Movie Night tonight," replied Dad. "One of the nice things about a staycation is resting and relaxing. After all, we're on vacation. We'll rent some DVDs and make popcorn after dinner."

"And look," said Mom, opening up a cupboard. "They were having a sale at BuyMore-PayLess, and I got giant plastic cups for our sodas."

"Tomorrow we thought we'd go to the Empire State Building," added Dad, "and then walk across the Brooklyn Bridge."

"Excellent!" said Lexie. "I haven't been to the Empire State Building since I was a little kid. Hey, I have an idea. You know that article on the pastel portraits at the Met? Could we spend a whole *day* at the Met? There's so much to see. Pearl, you'd like that, wouldn't you? I mean, it's an *art* museum and all."

It's true that I like art(s and crafts), but I was pretty sure there wasn't going to be an exhibit of sock monkeys at the Met. I didn't want to hurt anyone's feelings, though, since I'd been doing an awful lot of that lately, so I said, "Oh, yes!" and tried to sound sincere.

After breakfast, since it was vacation, Mom and Dad made coffee and sat in the family room and read the paper, spreading it out all over everything and looking as happy as if they were actually in an old hotel in the Wild West. Dad's cell phone rang and he didn't answer it. A package arrived at our door and Mom looked at it and said, "It's work," and stuck it on her desk without opening it.

Lexie didn't even bother to get dressed. "I'm going to spend the whole day in my pajamas," she announced, and she looked as happy as Mom and Dad.

I was already dressed and I don't enjoy reading the paper (or anything else) so for a while I just lay on the family room floor patting Bitey. Finally he bit me, so then I said, "I'm bored," and everyone looked at me in alarm.

"Get out your art supplies," suggested Dad.

"Call JB and see how he's feeling," said Mom.

"Write a postcard to Daddy Bo and tell him about our staycation," said Lexie.

"I don't have any postcards," I replied. "Could I walk to the corner by myself and buy some at Steve-Dan's?"

"No," said both of my parents.

"I'll go with you," Lexie offered.

I shook my head. "That's okay. I'll write him a letter."

I went to my room, closed my door a little louder than was truly necessary, sat at my desk, and began a note:

> Dear Daddy Bo,
> We are suposedly on vacation, but if we were really on vacation I would be seeing cactuses and rattlesnakes outside my window right now instead

of a brick wall. Oh by the way yesterday I broke JBIII's elbow.

Of course I didn't send the note. I didn't even finish it. I wadded it up and added it to the twenty-four apology letters in the wastebasket. I was sitting grumpily at my desk, my chin resting in my hand, not doing a single thing, when I heard a knock on my door and Lexie called, "Can I come in?"

"Don't you mean 'May I'?" I asked.

The door opened and Lexie waltzed in, sat on my bed, pointed at the spot next to her, and said, "Sit," which of course reminded me of treating JBIII like a dog.

"Pearl," she said, "I know you're upset about JBThree and that you're mad because we can't go on our trip. But could you stop and think about Mom and Dad for a minute? They feel bad about our trip, too, and they feel even worse thinking that they've disappointed us. Not to mention that Dad already feels bad about losing his job. You know what? It's kind of like you and I have a job now, and our job is to not make things worse than they are. When you moon around the apartment because you wish we were going on our trip instead of taking a staycation, it reminds Dad of the reason we have to stay at home."

I dropped my head and stared at a wrinkle in the bedspread.

"Mom especially needs this vacation," Lexie went

on. "She has to do more work now to try to make up for Dad's salary. She talked to her editor and she's going to write a whole series of books. Plus do some other things. So she's going to be really busy as soon as she goes back to work. Mom's pitching in, and we have to help, too. The least we can do is not complain.

"As for JBThree," my sister went on, "why don't you just call him? You'd feel better if you talked to him."

I shrugged.

"Well, could you please be grown-up about the staycation? Mom and Dad are doing their best. They're planning all sorts of things for us. I think we're even going to go out to dinner one night. You don't want them to feel bad, do you? It isn't like they're doing this to punish us. They couldn't help that Dad got fired."

"I know," I said at last.

"At least pretend to have fun, okay?"

I looked at Lexie and managed to put a smile on my lips, a real smile. "Okay."

Lexie smiled back at me. "Start with not acting bored today. Come on. This is summer vacation. No school! You'd better take advantage of it. You have a whole free day."

This was true. When it was February and I'd been in school for months and months and couldn't wait for summer vacation, I didn't want to remember today and think that I'd wasted it.

Lexie went back to lounging around in her pajamas, and I emptied my bank, walked into the family room, and said (smiling), "I'm taking your suggestion, Dad. I'm going to get out my crafts supplies. But first could we go to Steve-Dan's? There's something I really want, and I have enough money for it."

Dad could have been rude (like me) and said, "Are you sure you won't be embarrassed to be seen in public with your father?" But instead he said, "That sounds like fun. I'll be ready in a minute."

So Dad and I walked to the crafts store, where I bought a box of brads shaped like flowers to use for what is called "embellishing" when you're making cards or scrapbook pages, and on the way home I held Dad's hand even though that is not something an almost–fifth grader normally does, but I figured probably no one from my class would see us.

I spent all morning working on my summer scrapbook, except for when I got caught spying on Lexie. I was taking a little break from the scrapbook when I walked by Lexie's room and heard her talking and couldn't help peeking through her mostly closed door. The first thing I noticed was that my sister was sitting at her desk wearing her pajama bottoms with a very nice new blouse. I was about to ask about her suspicious outfit when I noticed another thing, which was that her computer was on and Liam's face was grinning out at Lexie. They were Skyping.

Lexie's back was toward me, so I stood and watched.

". . . Movie Night tonight," my sister was saying to her new boyfriend. "Tomorrow I probably won't be able to talk to you during the day because we're going to go to the Empire State Building and then walk across the Brooklyn Bridge."

"Cool," said Liam, and suddenly I realized why my sister was wearing a blouse. It was because she didn't want her boyfriend to see her pajamas.

I was storing this up to maybe tell JBIII if we were ever friends again, when I heard Liam say, "Who's that?"

"Who's who?" Lexie replied.

"That person peeking into your room."

Lexie whirled around. "Pearl!" she cried.

Uh-oh. I had forgotten that the Skype camera could see me, even if Lexie couldn't.

"Hi, Liam!" I said brightly. "It's me, Pearl, from the Camp Merrimac Starlettes. Sorry. I just wanted to ask Lexie a question, but it can wait until later." I closed the door in a hurry and hoped that by the time Lexie and her boyfriend were done, Lexie would have forgotten about my behavior (which that is exactly what happened).

The rest of the day passed and by the end of it my scrapbook was looking pretty good, and also my mind had been taken off of JBIII, except that I wished I had a friend to talk to. And no, I do not mean a boyfriend, although it did seem a little unfair that among the many things Lexie possessed—computer, cell phone, etc., etc., etc.—was a true and honest boyfriend. I just wanted someone I could call up and discuss the staycation with. I could have phoned Justine, I guess, but I would have had to start the conversation by defining "staycation" for her, and sometimes things like that take a while.

By dinnertime everyone had had a very nice day. Mom and Dad said we could have a picnic supper on the family room floor (a true picnic supper with everything laid out on a checked tablecloth, not just me crouched over a pile of dishcloths, trying not to spill). So we did, and after that, Movie Night began. Dad made popcorn and Mom got out the enormous movie-theater soda cups. She had also bought two giant-sized boxes of candy when she'd rented the DVDs, and we lay on the floor with our refreshments and watched three movies in a row—*Shrek*, *The Wizard of Oz*, and last of all, something called *Wuthering Heights*, which Lexie cried through and I fell asleep in the middle of.

The next day we became New York City tourists. After breakfast, we left our apartment and walked up Fifth Avenue until we came to the Empire State Building at 34th Street. We rode an elevator to the 102nd floor, which is the highest floor of the building, and learned that we were

1,250 feet above the ground, almost one quarter of a mile. Also, we learned that the Empire State Building was completed in 1931 and that it is the third-tallest skyscraper in the United States and the fifteenth tallest in the world. We walked around and around, and I looked out at all the shorter buildings like I was a hawk flying through the air. The people on the streets were as teensy as specks of pepper.

"Maybe we can see our apartment building from up here!" I shouted to Lexie. (It was very windy 102 stories in the air.)

We looked and looked, and counted the streets down to our block, but couldn't find our building.

Lexie took a million pictures with her cell phone and said she would print some out so that I could put them in my scrapbook. We stopped at the gift store on the way back down and Mom and Dad bought T-shirts for Lexie and me. When we were in the bright sunlight on Fifth Avenue again we bought sandwiches at a little café and ate outside, and I pretended we were in Paris and said "*Merci beaucoup*" to the waiter when he served me my grilled cheese sandwich.

Our day wasn't over yet. Next we took the subway downtown and found the entrance to the Brooklyn Bridge, which in case you didn't know, is over 125 years old and is one of the oldest suspension bridges in the United States. It spans the East River and is just a little more than a mile long, connecting Manhattan and Brooklyn. We walked slowly to the middle of the bridge, and for the second time that day I felt like a bird as we looked down at the water far below and at the tiny buildings ahead of us and behind us.

We walked and walked, and when we reached Brooklyn, I said, "Now what do we do?"

And Dad replied, "We go to the Brooklyn Ice Cream Factory."

Well. That sounded like fun. And it was. Sitting at the base of the Brooklyn Bridge with a vanilla milk shake was almost like being in another country. Suddenly I could sort of see the point of a staycation.

We finished our ice cream and then we walked around Brooklyn for a while, but finally we got tired so we took the subway back to Manhattan.

"Mom, Dad," said Lexie on the way home, "this was the best day ever!"

"It was great!" I added. "I can't wait to get back to my scrapbook."

But as it turns out I was a little tired from our adventures and took a two-hour nap when we got home. The next morning, I was ready for Day Three of our staycation.

VII. My family went on a lame staycation.
   A. We pretended to be tourists in our own city.
   B. Even though we were on vacation, I mean
      staycation, my sister got an idea about becoming
      a working girl.

One thing about my parents is that when they say they're going to do something they really mean it. They said we were going to be tourists in our own city, and they meant it. I thought our staycation had gotten off to a slow start, what with that first day of newspapers and pajamas and plastic movie cups. But by Day Three I had so much to put in my scrapbook that I barely had time to think about JBIII or our Wild West adventure that had tragically disappeared into the sunset.

Here are the highlights of the rest of our week:

MONDAY

We spent the entire day in Central Park. I had no idea there was so much to see and do in the park, since mostly we just nip into one end of it if we happen to be uptown for some reason, like if I need to have my teeth cleaned at Dr. Rice's office, which is on East 57th Street, or if Mom has taken me to FAO Schwarz, which is a fancy toy store that Lexie is embarrassed to be seen near, but that I still like very much. It turns out that there's a lot more to Central Park than the zoo, which I've been to a few times. For starters, the park takes up 843 acres, and in case you don't know how big that is, it's a rectangle that is two and a half miles long and half a mile wide, so you can imagine how much stuff you could fit in that space.

We found out an awful lot about Central Park by taking a guided tour of it that lasted two hours. When the tour was over, I said, "Can we go back to the zoo and see the penguins?" and Lexie said, "Can we go back to Belvedere Castle?" and Mom said, "I didn't see the statue of Alice in Wonderland," and Dad said, "I'm feeling a little peckish," which it turns out meant he was hungry, not that he was about to barf.

So first we bought hot dogs from a vendor and carried

them to the pond by the boathouse, and ate there while we watched kids sailing their model boats around the pond, something Lexie said she remembered reading about in *Stuart Little*, which sort of made me want to read the book, but not enough to actually decide to do it.

Then we went to the castle, which is very realistic-looking and was built in 1869, but not for anyone to live in, just for show. And here's something interesting: There is weather equipment on top of the castle now, so when a TV weather lady says what the temperature is in Central Park, she means the temperature on top of Belvedere Castle. This is true.

After the castle we found the Alice statue, and it turns out that unlike statues in museums, which have barriers around them because they're ancient and precious and the museum officials don't want any fingerprints on them, you're allowed to climb on Alice. Really. Of course, I was the only one in my family who climbed on her. My parents just admired her and fondly recalled reading the book (which I also decided not to read), and Lexie said the statue was creative and imaginative and she wondered a lot of dreamy, artistic things about the sculptor.

Finally we walked back to the zoo, where I watched the penguins for a while and Lexie said they reminded her of the book *Mr. Popper's Penguins*, and I truly hoped no one would get any ideas about summer reading for me.

TUESDAY

Our first stop was the Statue of Liberty, which I went to once on a field trip in second grade, but all I remembered about that trip was that we got to eat our lunches on the ferry on the ride home. This time I paid a little more attention. The statue was a gift to our country from the country of France in 1886. It was created by a sculptor named Frederic Bartholdi. The whole statue including the pedestal is 305 feet tall, but the lady herself is just 151 feet tall, which is still about $\frac{1}{32}$nd of a mile. The statue's head—just her head—was on exhibit at the World's Fair in Paris in 1878, which must have been a little bit creepy.

Guess what. The Statue of Liberty is another statue you're allowed to touch. In fact, you're allowed to climb up inside her all the way to her crown. Sadly, you have to make reservations months ahead in order to do that, and since months ago my dad was still teaching economics and wasn't a fired person and we were still going to fly out to the Wild West in August, all we could do was stand at the bottom of the statue with the other people who hadn't planned ahead and crane our necks back until we saw the crown from the outside. But that was still pretty impressive. I made a point of grinning at my family so they would see that I wasn't disappointed and that I was enjoying the staycation after all.

Our next stop was the Liberty Science Center, which is in the same general area as the Statue of Liberty, and is like a museum of fun, with all sorts of science exhibits and things you can experiment with and touch and climb, *plus* an IMAX theater where you can see very exciting movies about, for instance, tornadoes that look like they're going to whirl out into the audience. I had to shut my eyes a few times during the movie.

WEDNESDAY

This was a quieter day, which was good, since I was a little tired from all the sightseeing. Everyone slept late including Bitey and me, and then instead of a breakfast of BASICS rice cereal (which is a cheap version of Rice Krispies and hisses instead of crackles, and also doesn't have elves on the box) and BASICS bread and BASICS orange juice, we went to the Daily Grind for brunch. We sat at a little round table and Mom and Dad let Lexie and me order whatever we wanted, so of course Lexie ordered a Mocha Moxie with her food, and when I asked if I could have one, too, Mom and Dad looked at each other and then said yes. It turns out that coffee isn't all it's cracked up to be, even when it's served under a mountain of whipped cream. But no one said anything about my watering eyes, or the fact that I left most of the Moxie untouched. I concentrated on my seasonal fruit salad that was served in an elegant parfait glass, which everyone was afraid I would break.

What we were going to do next was a surprise for

Lexie and me. Mom and Dad had planned the adventure but wouldn't tell us about it ahead of time. So when we all got on the subway at Fourteenth Street my sister and I had no idea where we were going. We got off in midtown and followed Mom and Dad for a few blocks, and the next thing I knew we were standing in front of Madame Tussauds, which is a wax museum, but really so much *more* than a wax museum. There is also "Scream," a scare experience with real live people, who, let me tell you, are a lot scarier than wax people, and a 4-D movie theater where you can not only see and hear a movie but feel and smell things, such as ocean spray and chocolate. Some of those things, I'm sorry to say, were on the gross side, like this one smell that I thought was the smell that wafts off of a garbage truck. But Madame Tussauds was so much fun that it was almost as good as being in a ghost town or riding the range. I didn't want the afternoon to end.

THURSDAY

Well, if the trip to Madame Tussauds was one of my favorite events of the staycation, the event on Thursday was one of Lexie's. We spent the day at the Metropolitan Museum of Art.

The entire day.

Inside one building.

And I didn't see a single sock monkey. There were

some interesting beaded things and pieces of pottery, and thank *goodness* the museum also has a cafeteria and a gift shop, but how Lexie could get so very, very excited about, for instance, an exhibit called *The Renaissance Portrait from Donatello to Bellini* is beyond me. But I kept remembering Lexie's words about how our job was to not make things worse for our parents than they already were, so I pretended the hours in that museum were just fabulous, and as we were leaving I even said, "Oh, do we really have to go?" But when Dad said, "Of course not. Is there something else you'd like to see, Pearl?" I answered very quickly, "No, I just can't believe how fast the day went by," which was the opposite of the truth, but whatever. And then I ran down the museum steps before Dad could turn around and go back inside.

The night was a relief because we went out to dinner at a restaurant called Cowgirl Hall of Fame, where there's cowgirl stuff all over the walls and you can order food with names like Bar-k's Stockyard Hangar Steak and Branding Iron BBQ Chicken, and also buy prairie bead bracelets at the General Store that you walk through before you get to the restaurant part.

FRIDAY

Something so wonderful happened on Friday that it's too bad it wasn't the very last thing we did on our staycation. It would have been a great way to end our adventures. But as I have learned, things don't always happen the way you want them to.

On Friday morning Mom walked into the family room, yawned so widely that I knew it was a fake yawn, and said to Lexie and me, "Well, your dad and I haven't planned anything for the day. We'll just relax, okay?"

Right away I realized that Dad wasn't around, so I said, "Where's Dad?"

And Mom tried to lie and say she didn't know, but a parent always knows where the other parent is, so her reply ("Goodness, isn't he here in the apartment?") made me totally suspicious.

Dad came back that afternoon looking very proud of himself, pulled an envelope out of his pocket, and handed it to Lexie and me (the envelope, not his pocket).

Lexie opened the envelope and before I could say, "Hey! I wanted to open that," she started shrieking and running around the family room.

"What is it? What is it?" I cried.

"Tickets to *Amazing!* We're going to a Broadway show!" She shrieked again, then studied the tickets, and added, "Tonight! We're going tonight!"

"Count the tickets," said Dad with a smile.

Lexie counted. "Five," she reported.

Daddy Bo was going to go to the theater with us, which made the evening perfect.

It was the best surprise of the staycation.

SATURDAY

Spent day at Museum of Natural History, scene of biggest embarrassment of my life as student at Emily Dickinson. Refused to go anywhere near dinosaur wing. That's all you need to know.

And then it was Sunday, the last day of our staycation. My parents had not planned anything, saying that we needed to wind down. Another day of resting and relaxing before Mom started her new writing schedule and Dad went back to job hunting. I wondered what the last weeks of August would be like, with no Camp Merrimac, no staycation, and no JBIII.

I realized that I felt a little nervous.

"Lexie?" I said, peeping into her room.

My sister was sitting at her desk with her computer on. She was about to Skype with Liam. I knew this because she was wearing brown plaid pajama bottoms, socks with holes in them, and a freshly ironed pink and lime green top that Valerie had said showed off her bust, which means bosoms. I hoped my sister wouldn't have to get up from her desk for any reason, because then Liam would get a look at the lower half of her.

"Yeah?" Lexie swiveled around in her chair.

"Um," I said.

"Yeah?"

What I had meant to talk to Lexie about was my

nervousness, so I was surprised to hear myself say, "I have an idea. Let's make dinner for Mom and Dad tonight. A fancy dinner. They did so much for us this week, and now we can do something for them."

"Pearl, that's a wonderful idea!" is a comment people don't often make to me. But Lexie said it now. Then she switched off her computer and frowned thoughtfully. "Of course, we don't really know how to cook...."

"We could fix something, though. And we could ask Dad if it would be all right to clear his desk and then we could put out a tablecloth and nice napkins and the fancy china, and we could even light candles."

"And you could make a menu!"

We got right to work. We told Mom and Dad we had a surprise for them and that we needed the apartment to ourselves for a couple of hours in the afternoon. While they were gone we went through the refrigerator and the cupboards, and in the end I made up a menu that I thought was better than the one at Ollie's:

~DINNER SPECIAL~
PEARL AND LEXIE'S CAFÉ

☆ Orderves: saltines with chedder cheese
slices
☆ Beverage: ginger ale or water or whatever
you want
☆ Main Course: freezer pizza with salad a la
Lexie
❀ Note: We have two pizzas so you can
have three or four slices if necessary
☆ Dessert: chocolate chip cookies and
vanilla ice cream
☆ Also available: after-dinner coffee for
anyone except Pearl

Mom and Dad got dressed up for dinner, so then
Lexie and I did, too. We sat at the table in the family
room, which was set with dishes we hadn't used since
Easter, and ate our freezer pizza by the glow of candles.

"Isn't this just like in a restaurant?" I said, even though
it was nothing at all like Cowgirl Hall of Fame.

"Better!" Mom replied.

"I love the menu," added Dad.

The menu was propped up against a bottle of salad

dressing. I looked at it fondly. I had decorated the corners with the embellishments I had bought at Steve-Dan's a week earlier. They hadn't gone to waste.

We sat and sat and sat at the table, long after the cookies and ice cream were gone and Mom and Dad had each polished off two cups of coffee. No one wanted the staycation to end. And I didn't want to clean up the kitchen, but cleaning up was part of the dinner surprise, so finally Lexie and I got to work, and Mom and Dad disappeared into Mom's office.

It was later, when the kitchen was spotless and the dining room table had been turned into Dad's desk again, that I passed the closed door to the office and began to wonder why my parents were still in there. I glanced down the hall. Lexie was in her room Skyping with Liam. I paused. Then I pressed my ear to the office door.

"If my editor will agree to change the series deal to six books instead of four," Mom was saying, "that would make a big difference. And I talked to Patti about writing articles and reviewing books."

"How are you going to have time for all that?" asked Dad.

"I'm not sure," said Mom, which was not the answer I was hoping to hear, since there was this edge of nervousness to her words.

"There's a good chance I'll be out of a job until at least January," Dad said, and it sounded as though it was something he had already said several times, because it was followed by a long sigh. Then he added, "More likely, I'll be out of work until the beginning of the next school year. Although you never know."

I realized I couldn't hear Lexie anymore, which meant she had probably said good-bye to Liam. I sprang away from the office door. And just in time. Lexie poked her head into the hall.

"What are you doing?" she asked.

I decided to be honest for once. "Eavesdropping," I hissed, pushing Lexie back into her room and closing the door behind us.

I told her what I had heard.

Lexie sat at her desk chair. She rubbed her eyes. "Okay," she said. "Okay. Then it's time."

"For what?"

"For me to look for work. I'll start tomorrow."

"You're going to become a working girl?"

"I have to."

I frowned. Why did Lexie always get to be the mature sister?

But I didn't say anything. I left her room quietly, passed the office with my parents' voices drifting out of it, and stood at the window in our family room. I looked across the street. JBIII's apartment was dark.

VIII. My sister and I went job hunting.

A. Lexie got all the jobs.

The next morning I woke up at my usual summer hour of 5:00, switched on the light, and began a search of my closet. Six years ago, when Lexie and I were eight and four, Daddy Bo invited us to his house in New Jersey for Easter weekend. Just us girls, no Mom and Dad. He planned to take us to an Easter egg hunt on Saturday, and to church and out for brunch on Sunday. Since we never go to church, we didn't have appropriate clothes, so Mom popped Lexie and me in a cab and we rode to Lord & Taylor, where Mom bought us matching dresses (yellow with daisies) and straw hats decorated with yellow ribbons. We had outgrown the dresses years ago

(I gave mine to Justine), but my hat was still in the closet. Somewhere.

I kicked aside several pairs of shoes and a box that turned out to be my old Chutes and Ladders game and a green plastic bag that had fallen on something else, which turned out to be the missing bubble blaster, and finally, hanging on a peg behind my shirts, I saw the Easter hat. I stepped out of the closet and tried it on. Apparently your head grows a lot in the six years between when you're four and when you're ten because the hat instantly slid off. It landed on Bitey, which terrified him, and he shot out of my room and down the hall to the kitchen where he jumped onto the counter and crashed into the coffeemaker.

I paused for a moment, listening, but I didn't hear any other sounds. No one had woken up. I picked the hat up and jammed it on my head, and it popped back up like toast out of a toaster. So I put it on for a third time and pulled the fraying elastic band under my chin. The band was way too tight, but at least the hat stayed on.

I wanted to look nice for my first day of job hunting. On *I Love Lucy* when Lucy and Ethel decide to go job hunting they get all dressed up in suits and high heels and hats. I didn't have a suit or high heels, so I put on the outfit I'd worn when I won first prize in the art exhibit. Then I waited for Lexie.

I thought I might have to wait all the way until 11:00,

but Lexie got up in a big hurry at 8:30, and at 9:00 she ran into the kitchen for a bowl of cereal. She saw me sitting at the little table, wearing my pink shirt and pink skirt and yellow-ribboned Easter hat, my thumbs hooked through the elastic band to keep it from leaving a red mark under my chin.

"What's with the outfit?" she asked.

I ignored her. "How come you're wearing shorts?" Lexie's job-hunting outfit was a T-shirt, sandals, and a pair of shorts that were *so* short they could have been the bottom half of a bathing suit. "I thought you were going to look for a job today."

Lexie had been rummaging through our cupboard of BASICS food. She whipped around to face me. "SHHH!" She glanced into the family room, where Dad was sitting at his computer. "That's supposed to be a secret."

"What is? Job hunting? Why?"

Lexie rolled her eyes and hauled me out of the kitchen and into her room. "(A), I don't know if Mom and Dad will want me to go around looking for work, so (b), I want to *surprise* them tonight with all the jobs I find."

I frowned. "What?" I said finally.

Lexie shook her head. "Never mind. Anyway, what do shorts have to do with job hunting?"

"We're supposed to look nice when we apply for jobs."

Lexie was silent for so long that I think she might have been counting to ten or higher. At last she drew in a deep breath. "(A)," she said again, "we don't have to *apply* for jobs, and (b), I didn't realize you were coming with me."

"Well, I am."

Now there was a twelve- to fifteen-second pause. "*I* will be wearing *shorts* when *I* look for work. If you insist on following me around, you can. But I don't think anyone is going to want to hire a ten-year-old."

I shrugged. "I think otherwise," I said in a Mrs. Mott sort of voice. I flicked a yellow ribbon out of my eyes and stalked into my own room.

Lexie and I left our apartment together at 9:30. Dad didn't look up from his computer so he didn't see that I was wearing a job-hunting outfit.

"Where do you go to get jobs?" I asked my sister as we rode the elevator to the lobby.

"I don't know about you, but I'm going to start on the first floor and work my way up."

"The first floor of our apartment building?"

"Yes."

"I thought you were going to a job-placement agency." What I didn't say was that I had thought she was going to a job-placement agency like Lucy Ricardo and Ethel Mertz did when they needed to prove a point to their husbands in 1952.

"No."

Lexie's answers were getting awfully short, and I

thought it was because she didn't want to admit that a job-placement agency probably wouldn't be interested in a fourteen-year-old.

But all I said was, "No one lives on the first floor."

"No, but John's at the desk, and I need to talk to him."

We stepped off the elevator, and I ducked into the alcove where the mailboxes are, in order to avoid Mrs. Olson, who was hurrying through the lobby with Jasper and her flute case. When the coast was clear, I joined Lexie at John's desk.

". . . looking for summer jobs," my sister was saying. "You know, baby-sitting, dog-walking, that kind of thing. Would it be all right if I put up an ad by the mailboxes?"

"If it's all right with your parents it's all right with me," John replied.

"I might put one up, too," I said casually.

Lexie glared at me, then turned back to John and rolled her eyes at him like I wasn't standing right next to her with eyes of my own that could see her rolling eyes perfectly well. "I think it will be all right with Mom and Dad," said Lexie, after an eight-second pause in the conversation. "I'll check with them later, though, okay?"

"Okay," John replied. "Good luck. Good luck to you, too, Pearl."

"Thank you!" I said.

I followed Lexie to the elevator and we rode it to the second floor. Lexie hesitated outside the door of #2A, which is the first apartment I would have tried since, hello, it is #2A and it made sense to me to ring the door-bells in alphabetical order so you could keep track of where you had been. But Lexie decided to start with #2B, since she has a little crush on Mr. Berman, who lives in #2A. (Mr. Berman = handsome saxophone player, except for the mole on his eyelid.)

I was just thinking that maybe *I* should ring Mr. Berman's bell (I could hear him practicing, so I knew he was home) when the door of #2B opened and a tiny old lady who I think is named Mrs. Ledbetter smiled up at Lexie.

"Hello, dear," she said in that way old people have of saying "dear" when they've forgotten your name.

"Hi," said Lexie. "Um, how are you?"

"Just fine, dear."

I abandoned Mr. Berman's door in order to hear how a job-hunting conversation should go.

"That's *won*derful," said Lexie in a tone of voice I had never heard her use. "Well, I'm here because I'm looking for some jobs this summer—you know, so I won't get bored or anything—and I was wondering if you had any work for me. I could water your plants if you're going on vacation, or—" Here Lexie peered inside the apartment and she must have seen a cat because the next thing she said was, "Or come downstairs and feed your cat. I live in Seven F," she reminded Mrs. Berman.

"So do I," I said from behind Lexie.

"Are you both looking for work?"

"Yes," I replied.

"But I'm fourteen and going into high school," Lexie said. "Pearl here is only ten. Just so you know," Lexie rushed on, "I'm old enough to baby-sit and pet-sit, and I can give violin lessons, and also I'm a capable tutor of basic math, algebra, French, and Spanish."

"My," said Mrs. Ledbetter. She turned to me. "And what can you do?"

I thought for a moment. "I can draw."

Mrs. Ledbetter reached around Lexie and patted my hand. Then she turned back to my sister. "As a matter of fact," she said, "I'm going to be away the week after next, and I'd love to hire you to take care of Percy and water the plants. I'll give you the key to my mailbox, too, so you can bring the mail upstairs."

I don't know what the proper reaction to a job offer is, but Lexie just smiled and said, "Thank you." Then she pulled a pad of paper out of her pocket, made some notes on it, and asked Mrs. Ledbetter for her phone number. "I'll be in touch in the next day or two to firm things up," she added.

At #2C no one answered the bell. At #2D Mr. and Mrs. Baxter came hurrying through their door before Lexie could even ring the bell, saying that they were both late for work, which they certainly must have been since it was almost ten o'clock.

"I'll come back," Lexie called after them as they ran down the hall. "I was just wondering if you needed to hire me for anything. I can walk dogs and baby-sit—"

"Great! We need a sitter! I'll call you tonight," said Mrs. Baxter as the elevator doors opened. "Hi, Pearl," she added. "Nice to see you." And the doors closed.

This was pretty much the way the rest of the morning went. Lexie offered her services to our neighbors, and our neighbors smiled fondly at me and then asked Lexie if she could fit baby-sitting into her schedule. Or plant watering or grocery shopping or helping their children brush up on their arithmetic before school started again. Lexie asked for information and took notes and gave out her cell phone number.

"Would you like my number?" I asked Mr. Horowitz, who was a professor who had not been fired, and who had just offered Lexie the job of cleaning out his storage unit in the basement.

Mr. Horowitz looked confused. "I don't think I'll need it, will I?"

"Of course not!" said Lexie, laughing her fake adult laugh.

We had worked our way through the apartments on the sixth floor when I remembered something. "Hey, Lexie," I said, "you never went to Mr. Berman's apartment."

"Well, I didn't want to disturb his practicing. I'll go

back some other time." Lexie stepped onto the elevator and pushed the button for our own floor.

We had to be a little careful on our floor because of course we didn't want Mom or Dad to see us. Lexie glanced at our door, then rang the bell at #7D, which used to be Justine's apartment. A couple with a baby named Matthew had moved into it a few months after Justine's family had moved out. That had been disappointing since I had been hoping for a girl neighbor my age, not a boy neighbor in diapers. Lexie had immediately begun sitting for Matthew.

"Good morning!" said Lexie brightly when Mrs. Harmer answered the door, Matthew riding on her hip. "I'm just here to let you know that I'm available not only for babysitting but to do other jobs or chores. I can organize things, run errands, whatever you need."

"And I can—" I started to say, but at that very moment the elastic band under my chin finally broke and the Easter hat blasted off of my head and hit Etienne in the face as he stepped out of the service elevator.

Etienne rubbed his eye, which had instantly turned red, Lexie looked more appalled than I had ever seen her, and Mrs. Harmer began to laugh.

"Pearl," said Lexie warningly.

"I'm sorry, Etienne. It was an accident. Here." I handed him a tissue from the pocket of my pink skirt. Etienne held it to his eye as I ran to our apartment. Lexie had had enough of me.

I spent the afternoon in my room, working on my scrapbook, trying not to picture JBIII falling down on the dock at Camp Merrimac, and wondering how many more jobs Lexie had lined up. I found out at dinner.

"Mom, Dad," said Lexie as she and I sat on the floor of the family room, leaning against the couch with bowls of spaghetti in our laps, "I have something to tell you."

If *I* had said that, my parents would have looked at each other in alarm. But when Lexie said it, Dad just went, "Yes?"

"I didn't think I should spend the rest of the summer lying around, so I decided to find some work." Lexie set her bowl of pasta aside and reached for her notebook. "I talked to some of our neighbors today—"

"And she was *not* in a proper job-hunting outfit," I interrupted.

"—and I lined up a few jobs," Lexie continued as if I hadn't said anything at all. She consulted the notebook. "Let's see. I'm going to babysit for Matthew, Jude and Quinn, Trent, and the twins. And I'm going to pet-sit for Mrs. Ledbetter, clean out Mr. Horowitz's storage unit, give a violin lesson to Mrs. Mott's niece when she visits . . ." The list went on and on. "I'll be earning my own money now."

"Lexie, that's wonderful!" exclaimed Mom.

"I'm so proud of you," said Dad.

I didn't add a compliment of my own. But I made a decision. The next morning I would go job hunting by myself. I would wear regular clothes, I would carry a notebook, and I would start off at Mr. Berman's apartment, since Lexie still hadn't found the nerve to go there. I realized that I needed to be clear about what I could offer to prospective clients, so as soon as we finished our floor-supper, I went to my room and sat at my desk with a blank piece of paper in front of me. At the top of the paper I wrote: Talents and Skills

I headed the list with: Art

I stared into space for a while. The very fact that I had to think for so long was humiliating. Finally I added Cat care to the list. I thought of Lexie's skills. I couldn't play an instrument. No one was going to hire a ten-year-old tutor, and most likely no one was going to trust me with the key to their apartment.

But you never knew.

VIII. My sister and I went job hunting.

   A. Lexie got all the jobs.

   B. I found out how it feels to be my father.

The next morning Lexie was out of bed at 8:00 and hurrying off to her first job by 8:45. She was supposed to be upstairs at the Petrowskis' apartment at 9:00 and it would only take her approx. twenty seconds to get there, but Lexie said she wanted to make a good first impression by arriving early.

"I hope they're dressed," I called down the hall after her.

Lexie shot me an annoyed glance and stepped onto the elevator.

My sister's first job was organizing the books in the

Petrowskis' shelf-filled living room. Their shelves start at the ceiling and go all the way to the floor, covering every inch of wall space in a very large room. And the books were all jumbled around (according to Lexie) and not in any particular order. The Petrowskis wanted them categorized and then arranged alphabetically according to the author's last name.

This sounded like a hideous homework assignment to me, but Lexie had headed off with relish. She hoped to finish the job by 3:00 that afternoon when she had an appointment to baby-sit for Jude and Quinn Bissell on the tenth floor.

My sister would be earning money all day long.

I would be job hunting again.

As I had planned, I wore regular clothes—shorts, a T-shirt, and my sneakers—and I stuck a notebook and a pencil in my pocket. I still wasn't sure what I could offer people, apart from my artistic talents and maybe cat care, but I hoped they would be able to think of some things.

I left the apartment at 9:00 and took the elevator to the second floor, where I rang the bell of #2A, even though I couldn't hear any saxophone bleats coming from inside. Mr. Berman opened the door right away, though.

"Good morning, Pearl," he said. "Isn't this a surprise."

I wasn't sure what to say to that, so I just went, "Hi," and tried not to stare at the mole on his eyelid.

"Can I help you with anything?" he asked.

I pulled the notebook out of my pocket. "I'm looking for work." I paused. "I need money. Do you have any jobs for me?"

Mr. Berman stared off into space. "Well, I could use an apartment-sitter, but I think that's a job for someone who's a bit older. I'm sorry."

"That's okay," I said. "Thanks anyway."

I skipped Mrs. Ledbetter's apartment since she had already given her job to Lexie, rang the bell at #2C, where once again no one answered, and then rang the Baxters' bell. Mrs. Baxter answered it in a hurry, stuffing her feet into high heels as she did so. She had probably gotten into trouble at her office for being so late the day before.

"I don't want to keep you," I said quickly, "but I was just wondering if you have any other baby-sitting jobs coming up. I'm available, too."

"All right. And you're how old?"

"Um, ten."

"Hmm. Well, it's just that the twins are only two years younger than you, honey. I think we need someone older."

Someone like Lexie.

I nodded. "Okay. Thanks."

I stuck to my plan of ringing doorbells in numerical and alphabetical order. Half an hour later, this is how many jobs I had lined up: zero. Here are the reasons no one wanted to hire me:

1. I was too young.
2. I couldn't drive. (Lexie wouldn't have gotten that job, either.)
3. I was too young.
4. I didn't know French.
5. I wasn't tall enough.
6. I was too young.
7. I couldn't sew.
8. I didn't have any computer skills.
9. I didn't have a cell phone.
10. I was too young.

I considered telling people I would work for free, but that seemed as pathetic as my two-item Talents and Skills list.

I took the service elevator back to the seventh floor and sat in the hallway outside our apartment for a while. I thought about my father. Was this how he felt when he applied for a job and was told he didn't have the right kind of experience? Or that somebody else had more experience or had taught at a bigger college or was older (or younger) than he was?

I had only been job hunting since yesterday and already I was frustrated and humiliated. My father had been job hunting for two months. Plus, he had a family he needed to help support. I just wanted to buy a hamster.

I rang a few more bells, got zero more jobs, and finally returned to our apartment at lunchtime. Dad was out somewhere. Mom was in her office with the door closed and an unfriendly DO NOT DISTURB sign hanging on the knob. And Bitey was asleep behind the couch and wouldn't even flick an ear when I called to him.

I fixed a sandwich and ate it on the couch without dish towels or paper towels or even a napkin, since I was in a bad mood.

Also, I was lonely.

I missed Justine. I missed JBIII. I even missed Lexie. I had no human friends.

After lunch I made a flyer just like the one Lexie had made (once she had gotten permission from Mom and Dad). In fact, I copied Lexie's flyer except for changing the word "Lexie" to the word "Pearl." And in the space in which my sister had listed her many, many skills I wrote:

CALL ME TO FIND OUT WHAT I CAN DO!

At the bottom of the sheet I made tear-off phone-number tabs, which the number was different from Lexie's, since my sister has her own personal cell phone and I don't. I didn't ask anyone at all for permission to make or hang the sign. I just tiptoed into the lobby, snuck over to the mailboxes while John was talking to the FedEx man, and hung my ad next to Lexie's. I was too mad to care what anyone thought about this. Then I went back to my apartment to wait for the phone to start ringing. It rang three times that afternoon, and each time my mother answered it in her office and didn't come out, so obviously no one was offering me any jobs. Just before dinner I checked my ad in the lobby. Maybe someone (and by someone I mean Lexie) had taken it down. But it was still hanging, and all the phone-number tabs were in place.

No one was interested in me. I was useless.

Plus, I was friendless.

And a little bored.

Being a working girl must have made Lexie feel unusually grown-up, because when we carried our plates of fried chicken and BASICS canned peas into the family room that evening, Lexie edged a couple of Dad's piles of paper aside and sat at the table with our parents. I was the only one sitting on the floor surrounded by dish towels.

Mom and Dad and I dug into the chicken. Lexie sat primly in her chair.

Finally Mom said nervously, "Lexie? Why aren't you eating?"

My sister began to smile. She reached into her pocket, pulled out a fistful of bills, and fanned them across the table.

Dad looked fondly at his older daughter. "Is that what you earned today?"

Lexie nodded.

"Goodness," said my mother. "That's quite a bit for your first day of work."

Lexie nodded again and said in a fake shy voice, "It's for you. For both of you. To help out." She pushed it toward them.

My mother immediately burst into tears. Then she put her hand to her mouth as if pre-barf, but she removed it right away. "Oh, honey. That's too generous." Her words were all wobbly.

My father cleared his throat five times before he managed to say, "We can't take your money. You earned that."

"Pearl and I use the money you earn," Lexie pointed out. "You always say it's for the family. Well, so is this." She edged the bills closer to our parents.

A tear slid down Mom's right cheek. Then a tear slid

down her left cheek. I felt like crying, too, but for different reasons. I had absolutely nothing to offer my parents.

I sat on the floor among the dish towels like the useless, jobless, friendless, skill-free, spill-prone person I was.

Over at the table Mom wiped her cheeks with her napkin, and my father dabbed at his eyes and cleared his throat again.

I kept my eyes on that pile of $$. I was very curious to find out where it was going to wind up. Lexie gave the bills one more little push, and then Dad pushed them back to her.

"You keep that, sweetie," he said.

"It really is yours," Mom added.

A thoughtful expression crossed my sister's face, like she was thinking about homework, or death. "All right," she said after a moment, and she stuffed the money back into her pocket. I was shocked. She had given in awfully easily. Lexie had probably staged this scene just to make herself look noble.

"I'll keep the money," Lexie said at last, "but you can stop giving me an allowance. I won't need one as long as I'm working."

"What?!" I cried. Everyone turned around and looked at me. "I mean, that's really nice of you, Lexie."

"Thank you," said my sister just as both of my parents rose from their seats and put their arms around her.

"You're growing up so fast," Mom whispered into Lexie's hair. "We're so proud of you."

"This is very, very generous," said Dad. "I can't tell you how much your gesture means to us."

"So," said Lexie, "you agree? No more allowance?"

"We agree," Dad replied.

"But once school starts," my mother said, "your home-work comes first. If you don't have enough time to earn money and keep up with your work then we'll give you your allowance back, okay?"

"Okay."

Probably ours was the only home in which the parents had to beg one of their children to take money from them.

I carried my plate into the kitchen, stalked down the hall to my room, and mentally slammed the door.

19

IX. I finally made up with JBIII.

During the week of our staycation my scrapbook had filled up nicely with all sorts of interesting observations, notes, photos, drawings, and mementos. Here is what I put in the scrapbook on Monday night after my first day of job hunting: 0

Here's what I put in the scrapbook on Tuesday night after my second day of job hunting: 0

Here's what I put in the scrapbook on Wednesday night after my first day of doing nothing at all: 0

Here's what I put in the scrapbook on Thursday night after my second day of doing nothing at all:

JOB-HUNTING PROGRESS		
	LEXIE	PEARL
# of job offers — Weds.	4	0
# of job offers — Thurs.	3	0
# of jobs completed — Weds.	2	0
# of jobs completed — Thurs.	3	0
Amt. of $$ earned	so much she can't even count it	0
Amt. of time wasted	0	all
# of phone number tabs removed from ad in lobby	8	0

I had posted my ad in the lobby on Tuesday afternoon. By Friday morning it was still hanging in a clean and tidy manner, while Lexie's ad was all gray and wrinkled from people fighting to tear off the tabs at the bottom. Only two of her tabs were left, and Lexie spent the better part of each day walking dogs and organizing storage units and burping babies and reminding kids about the commutative property.

221

Our apartment had become very, very quiet. My father went on several job interviews. When he was at home, he sat at his desk and researched articles he planned to write. I couldn't watch TV then because the TV was twelve inches from his computer and the cartoon clangs and boinks bothered him. Mom remained behind her closed office door with the sign hanging, which I think it was a little rude to leave the sign up for so long after she had already made her point about not wanting to be disturbed.

I made a paper necklace for Bitey that he immediately bit in two, and drew some pictures of Lexie carrying eleven shopping bags since she was so rich, and spent a lot of time staring out the family room windows at the windows of JBIII's apartment across the street. I never saw any signs of life over there. I was hoping to glimpse JBIII's head as he walked through their living room. Sometimes I sat downstairs in the lobby and spied on the lobby of the Brubakers' building. No sign of JBIII there, either. Maybe he was on vacation with his parents. I couldn't remember what the Brubakers' vacation plans were.

Or maybe JBIII was in the hospital, and that's why no one was at home. His parents were spending all their time with their severely injured son while he recovered from surgery to repair the damage caused by the son's former best friend, jobless Pearl Littlefield.

But that probably wasn't true. My parents had talked with JBIII's parents several times and I knew someone would have told me if JBIII was lying in a hospital bed, learning how to feed himself and hold a pencil again.

On Friday morning promptly at 8:45, my mother closed herself into her office, my father left the apartment dressed in a suit (suit = job interview), and Lexie left with him, on her way to walk Jasper for the Olsons. Breakfast was barely over and already I was bored. I considered snooping through Lexie's drawers but decided to go down to the lobby instead. Sometimes first thing in the morning, in nice weather, a policeman patrols our block on his bicycle and I always hope to see him get distracted by a flock of pigeons and crash into a fire hydrant. Then I could be the one to shout to John, "Emergency! Emergency! Call nine-one-one!"

I sat on the bench and looked around the lobby. It was very neat and clean. And dull. Nobody was in the little mailbox room. Nobody was checking the computer display on the front desk. John was busy talking to Etienne. Apparently, there was a problem with Mr. Graves in #10H, who kept leaving his keys in the lock on his door and then phoning down to John and saying the keys were missing and could John please, please organize a search of the building for them?

Mr. Thompson came in from walking Hammer, and John reached into the cabinet under the desk and pulled a Milk-Bone out of the box he keeps there for Hammer and Jasper and the other apartment dogs. Hammer took the treat delicately between his teeth and carried it to the elevator so that he could eat it in private later.

I looked outside again.

The policeman rode by wearing shorts and didn't go anywhere near a fire hydrant.

From the desk I heard Etienne say, "He has already called you five times zees morneeng?"

Mrs. Ledbetter left the building carrying a straw purse over her arm.

Mr. Berman returned to the building with a cup of coffee from the Daily Grind.

I was watching Mr. Berman hold the elevator door open for Mrs. Harmer, who was struggling with her pocketbook, a shopping bag, and Matthew in his stroller, when I heard a car door slam. I looked outside again. And there were JBIII and his mother getting out of a cab. I jumped to my feet and watched them walk into their building. JBIII didn't look too bad. He didn't even have a cast on his arm. In fact, he was moving pretty quickly.

After lunch that day my father banned me from the family room until I stopped singing a song I had written to the tune of "Mary Had a Little Lamb" that went like this: Lexie is a stuck-up queen, stuck-up queen, stuck-up queen. Lexie is a stuck-up queen, and she's very mean.

"Lexie isn't even here," my father called down the hall after me as I huffed into my room.

I sang the song loudly for fifteen minutes with Bitey as my audience and then I returned to the family room. My father eyed me over his glasses, but he didn't say anything and neither did I. I knelt against the back of the couch and looked across the street at JBIII's apartment.

It took me a couple of seconds to realize that JBIII was looking back at me.

I gave him a little wave, and he waved to me, a much bigger wave. Then he put a finger in the air, signaling me to wait, and disappeared from view. I sucked in my breath and didn't breathe again until he returned. When he did, he held up a sign that read: COME OVER?

I couldn't believe it. I grinned, signaled for *him* to wait, grabbed a piece of printer paper from Dad's desk, scribbled OKAY!!!! on it, and held it up for my friend to see.

I wasn't sure if he meant that he wanted to come over here or wanted me to go to his apartment, but I didn't wait to find out. I flew down to the lobby and was rushing past John's desk when I nearly collided with JBIII.

If JBIII was a girl I might have hugged him, but he wasn't, so I didn't.

For a few seconds we just looked at each other. Finally I said, "Want to go upstairs?"

He shrugged. "All right."

We walked back to the elevator and JBIII pushed the button with his right hand, which was a good sign.

"So you can feed yourself?" I asked.

"What?"

I pointed to his elbow. "You can use your arm okay?"

"Oh, sure," said JBIII, as if he had never been knocked down (by me) and been rushed off to a hospital.

"How long did you have to wear your cast?"

"Zero minutes. I never had one. Just a sling. And I don't have to use it anymore."

The elevator door opened and we stepped onto the seventh floor.

"You're kidding," I said.

"Nope."

Huh. I certainly must have a lively imagination.

We walked into my apartment and down the hall to my room where we sat on the floor, and before JBIII could get one word out, I said, "JBThree, I'm really sorry I ran into you and you got hurt. I felt horrible and I didn't know what to do. I was even afraid to apologize to you because I thought you were still mad about our fight. The weird thing is that when I was running after you on the dock it was because I wanted to say I was sorry for being so bossy." I hoped all this would show him how mature I'd become recently.

"Okay."

I also hoped this would be the end of the fight discussion. But it wasn't.

"Boy," JBIII went on, "I was really mad at you. Not about the accident. That was just an accident. But about the other stuff."

"Duh. And I was mad at you. But I am sorry I was bossy. I just wanted you to have a good time at Water-Works. I wanted to make sure you went on all the best rides and ate all the best foods. I guess I was showing off a little."

"A *little*?"

"Okay, a lot. But after that you really hurt my feelings. It was like you wanted to prove you didn't need me as a friend anymore."

JBIII stared at the wall. "I know. I'm sorry, too."

"Do you really still want me to be your friend?"

"Definitely."

"I missed you. I was bored."

"I missed you, too."

I noticed that JBIII didn't say he'd been bored.

"So what have you been up to?" I asked.

"Well, my parents and I went to Rhode Island to visit my aunt and uncle. And my mom found out about this kids' computer camp. I went to that every morning last week."

That was fine, but what I really wanted to know was whether JBIII had been hanging around with Jill.

"Huh," I said. "Interesting. So . . . do you like Jill?"

JBIII burst out laughing. "Jill Di*Nun*zio?"

That was all I needed to hear. I gave him what I think is called a sheepish smile, although I, personally, have never seen a sheep smile, so really it was just sort of an embarrassed smile. "Yeah."

"Nope," JBIII replied. "I do not." (Here is where Lexie would have said, "End of discussion.")

I studied JBIII's arm, which looked absolutely fine to me. "What happened with your elbow?" I asked at last. "Why didn't you get a cast?"

"I just didn't. The doctor said it wouldn't do any good, not the way the bone was broken. At first I was supposed to hold it still—that was when I wore the sling—and then I started doing physical therapy and the doctor said I didn't even need the sling anymore. When school starts I won't be able to take gym for a while, but that's it."

I thought JBIII sounded just the teensiest bit disappointed and I understood why. After all, it would be pretty exciting to start school with a giant cast on your arm. On the other hand, it would probably be better if the fifth graders at Emily Dickinson Elementary didn't know that I was the one who had knocked JBIII onto a canoe.

"What have you been doing?" asked JBIII.

I told him about our staycation and about the job hunt and how no one wanted to hire me because I was too young, too short, and couldn't drive, sew, or speak French.

"Aren't you forgetting something?" asked JBIII.

"Oh, yeah. I don't have a cell phone, either."

"I *mean*, that you're an artist."

"No one offered me any art jobs."

"Did you ask them if they *had* any art jobs?"

"No."

JBIII shook his head. "The thing about looking for a job is that you have to sell yourself."

"Have you ever looked for a job?"

"No, but . . ." He trailed off.

I had the uncomfortable feeling that JBIII might have overheard his parents talking about my father's search for a job. But I was desperate. "What do you mean, sell yourself?" I asked.

"You have to tell people what you're good at and then make them think they need your skill. Look. Pretend you live in this building."

"I do live in this building."

"I mean, pretend you're a grown-up in this building, and I come to your door. I'll be you, okay?"

JBIII stepped out into the hallway and said, "Ding-dong."

I got to my feet. "Hello, little girl," I said. "If you're here looking for work, don't bother. I don't hire children."

JBIII made a face. "Be serious. Just answer the door."

"Okay." I closed my door and opened it again. "Yes?"

"Hello. I was wondering if you have any stationery needs."

"What?"

"You know. Do you need any notepaper or invitations or greeting cards?"

"JBThree, what are you talking about?"

JBIII grinned at me. "I'm getting an idea," he said.

X. JBIII and I went into business.

A. JBIII got an excellent idea.

At exactly nine o'clock the next morning the phone rang and I jumped to answer it. It was Saturday, and Lexie didn't have any jobs lined up, so she was still asleep. My parents were in their pajamas, doing their favorite weekend thing: reading the paper and drinking coffee.

"Hello?" I said, walking the phone into the hallway, as if I had ever in my life gotten an important call that I had to take in private.

"Hi, it's me," said JBIII. "Can you come over?"

"Right now? Why?"

"Just come. And bring as much of your art stuff with you as you can carry."

"Why don't you come over *here?*"

"I have an idea for a business for us to go into. And we need my parents' computer and printer."

This was interesting. "What's the idea?"

"Come over and I'll show you."

I found a shopping bag wedged between the refrigerator and the kitchen cabinet, and I loaded it up with my papers and markers and ink pads and rubber stamps and embellishments and tubes of glitter and rolls of ribbon. I lugged the bag to our family room. "Going to JBThree's," I announced.

"Really?" my mother replied with an astonished smile on her face.

"Yeah. We made up. I apologized."

When I rang the bell at JBIII's apartment his father answered the door and just said "Hi," so I knew he thought it was safe for me to be around his son again.

"Pearl, come in here!" called JBIII from his parents' office.

FYI, here's what JBIII's parents do: Mrs. Brubaker has a job with a company in Seattle and does absolutely all of her work from her computer in New York City, except for every now and then when she has to fly across the country for a meeting. And Mr. Brubaker owns a store in a part of Manhattan called Soho, which I have never been to the store because all it sells is lamps.

I hurried into the office and set my bag on the floor.

"I brought everything," I said. "Well, almost everything. What's your idea?"

JBIII gestured to a table that he had set up like a display in a store: Arranged in two neat rows were a box of note cards, a stack of party invitations, some stationery, and a sheet of address labels.

"What's that?" I asked.

"Stuff my mom has bought. Stationery and cards and labels. And guess what?"

"What?"

"We could make all those things ourselves. In fact, we could do a better job. You know, make them fancier and more colorful."

"We could?"

JBIII nodded. "And that's my idea. Made-to-order stationery items. You'll design them, and I'll print them out. See?" JBIII sat down at the computer. "I can scan your artwork and then print in color. We'll get blank paper and cards and envelopes at Steve-Dan's. Sheets of blank labels, too. Then we'll ask people what they want and they'll say, like, invitations to my son's birthday party. And you'll go, what's the party theme? And they'll go, dinosaurs. So you'll design dinosaur invitations, which I'll print out. Then we'll package the invitations up nicely with envelopes."

"And sell them," I said. "JBThree, that's brilliant! But about buying the supplies—how will we know how many of each thing to buy? I mean, what if we don't earn back as much as we spend? Once? On *I Love Lucy*?" JBIII rolled his eyes, but I ignored him. "Lucy and Ethel went into business bottling and selling salad dressing and at first it seemed like a great idea because they went on TV to advertise their business and they got tons of orders, but it turned out they weren't charging enough for their salad dressing so they were losing money on each bottle, and Ricky and Fred got really mad."

JBIII looked calm and undisturbed. "One of the keys to our business," he said, "will be making sure we charge more money for the finished items than we spent buying the supplies. And we'll only buy what we need to fill our orders, nothing extra."

This was sounding better and better. "Hey!" I exclaimed. "After you've printed out the cards—or the invitations or whatever—I could add special touches to them. You know, like glitter or ribbons or sequins. Of course, we'd have to charge more for those items." I paused, frowning. "Huh. On the other hand . . ."

"On what other hand?" asked JBIII, looking slightly annoyed.

"Well, on the other hand, do you think people will really want to buy this stuff? After all, most people just send e-mail now. They don't write actual thank-you notes or send invitations anymore. They just type a few lines into their computers and click Send."

"Not everyone," said JBIII. "Plenty of people like to do things the old-fashioned way. Like my mom, who only reads real books. She says she will never, ever get into bed at the end of a long day with a piece of electronic equipment. She wants pages that she can hold in her hands. She likes turning the pages and imagining who else might have held the book and turned the pages before she did. She says she even likes the way books smell and that nothing will ever take the place of that. And I think lots of people would rather send a nice handmade card or invitation—one with colorful flowers—"

"Decorated with sequins!"

"—that someone could put up on their refrigerator and admire. Anyway," JBIII continued, "the very first thing we should do is make some samples to show our neighbors. Then we can take orders. If no one orders anything, well, it will be sad, but at least we won't have wasted any money. I have enough supplies here so that we can make samples."

So we set to work. JBIII found an old loose-leaf notebook and we replaced the lined paper that was in it with pieces of oaktag.

"We'll glue our samples on these pages and then we'll have a professional book to show our neigh—our customers," said JBIII. "Now, what should we put in the sample book?"

"How about two designs for notecards—maybe one

that says 'Thank You' on the front—and two designs for invitations and one design for address labels. And the art can be mix-and-match."

"What do you mean 'mix-and-match'?"

"Well, if someone likes the art on the address labels but wants it on invitations, we could do that. Any of the designs could go on any of our, um, products."

"Oh, that's good!" said JBIII admiringly. "Actually, if we use the designs that way, I can make up more than five samples."

I got out my markers and paper and by lunchtime our sample book was ready. I had drawn bumblebees and tulips, a mouse holding a piece of cheese in its front paws, and a simple vine of leaves and flowers like this:

And JBIII had used all the designs to make note cards, invitations, and labels. I had also designed a fancy pink-and-green THANK YOU, which he'd made into another notecard. We wanted to start taking orders right then, but we could both hear JBIII's stomach growling, which we thought might not be good for business, so we made peanut butter sandwiches and ate them in a big hurry before carrying the sample book into JBIII's living room.

"Mom, Dad," said my best friend, "you have the honor of being our first customers." We sat together on the couch, the sample book open across our laps, Mr. and Mrs. Brubaker on either side of us.

"These are lovely!" exclaimed Mrs. Brubaker as she examined our product lines. She said this in a genuine way, not in that way some grown-ups have of sounding all excited when you know that what they really mean is, "How pathetic. And look at all the trouble you went to. I guess I'll have to buy something out of pity."

"I'll say," agreed Mr. Brubaker, also in a genuine way.

And before we knew it, JBIII and I had taken our first orders—a box of the thank-you notes for Mrs. Brubaker, and a sheet of bee-and-tulip address labels for Mr. Brubaker, but with JBIII's mother's address on them.

"I guess we don't have any designs for men," JBIII whispered to me, and we decided to get to work on that as soon as we had time.

JBIII wrote down the orders on a notepad and then we closed the sample book and set off.

"Only go to the neighbors you know!" called Mr. Brubaker as JBIII and I stepped into the hall.

Our first stop was at the apartment next door, where a very old man seemed absolutely thrilled to see JBIII and me and ordered some mouse and cheese notecards for his granddaughter. Across the hall an annoyed-looking teenage boy answered the door and I knew right away we weren't going to make a sale and I was right. But down the hall in the apartment by the elevator a young couple ordered three sheets of address labels, and just as we were about to leave the man suddenly said, "Oh, wait! Emily, we should order invitations for Brielle's birthday party." And then the woman said, "The bumblebees are awfully cute." And I said, "I could hand-decorate them with glitter." And her eyes grew wide and she asked for twenty special-order invitations.

By the time we had visited people on the eighth, ninth, and tenth floors, we had taken orders for fourteen different items, including three special items that would be hand-decorated.

"This is amazing!" I exclaimed.

"Definitely. Okay. Let's stop here and go buy supplies."

"Stop here! Why? Everyone's ordering stuff. We should keep going."

"Nope. A good businessperson doesn't get in over his head," said JBIII, which was probably something he had heard his father the lamp salesman say from time to time. "We should fill these orders first, just to make sure we can actually do it, and also so we don't make anyone wait too long for their merchandise. Come on. Let's go to Steve-Dan's. How much money do you have?"

I gaped at my friend. "Zero."

"Oh."

"How much do *you* have?"

"Three dollars."

"How much do you think the supplies will cost?"

JBIII frowned up his face and did some arithmetic in his head while we waited for the elevator. "I'm not sure," he said finally, "but more than three dollars."

We went back to JBIII's apartment, where we found a calculator and figured out how much money we would need at the store, and then how much money we would have after we had filled our orders and gotten paid. If we borrowed some money from his parents we could pay them back quickly and still have a profit for ourselves.

"But remember, after this, we'll always have to use our earnings to buy supplies," said JBIII, which is the annoying kind of thing my father the economist would say.

"Yeah, but what's left over is just for us," I replied.

Like for investing in an iPod or a hamster.

The Brubakers weren't too thrilled with the idea of lending their son and me money until JBIII showed them our math. Then Mr. Brubaker drew up a document for us, which I think was his way of saying that even though we were kids he still expected to be paid back promptly. So we signed the paper with our best signatures:

Pearl Littlefield   *James Brubaker III*

And then JBIII said, "Can we go to the store by ourselves?" and his mother was like, no, and she came with us. BUT . . . when we reached the store, she said, "You know what? There's too much air-conditioning in there. I'll wait for you outside," and that was *her* way of giving us a little independence, since we were businesspeople with profits and good math.

In the store I lingered by the display of rubber stamps and then by some hot-glue guns and by a whole lot of other items that weren't on JBIII's shopping list, and finally he said, "If you want to buy any of those things you'll have to pay my parents back with your own portion of the profits," so then we just put blank notecards and invitations and sheets of labels in our basket and boringly paid for them.

Still, it was exciting when the salesman saw us shopping all by ourselves without an adult and I was able to say to him, "We've gone into business. We promise to buy all our supplies here. Do we get a discount?"

"Not a discount," he replied, "but a frequent shopper card." And he punched a little hole in the top of a plasticized card and handed it to us. "When you have ten holes punched in the card," he said, "you'll get ten percent off of your next purchase."

JBIII and I were officially in business.

X. JBIII and I went into business.

A. JBIII got an excellent idea.

B. I surprised my parents.

When JBIII and I returned to the Brubakers' office with our supplies it was late in the afternoon, but we got to work filling our orders anyway. JBIII said that responsible businesspeople wouldn't waste time and that we should keep our customers happy. I was just eager to start gluing glitter to the bees. Plus, I wanted my money.

By the time Mom phoned to tell me to come home for dinner, JBIII had printed out three sets of notecards and packaged them in tissue paper tied with ribbon, and I was nearly done with the glittery bumblebees. The cards were drying on every surface in the office, and if you must know the truth, I had sneezed and blown yellow glitter across the carpet, which JBIII said we would have to clean up before his parents saw it. And also that we should use newspapers the next time we got a glitter order. But we were happy with our progress and couldn't wait to get back to work the next morning.

On Sunday, without being asked, I showed up at the Brubakers' at 8:00 a.m. in the morning, which may have been a little early, because Mr. Brubaker was still in his pajamas, and he ran into the bedroom when he saw me. But JBIII and I were all businesslike and I didn't pay any attention to his father's GOT MILK? T-shirt with the giant rip in the underarm.

We just set to work, and an hour later JBIII announced, "Okay. All the seventh-floor orders have been filled. Let's deliver them."

"Shouldn't we finish the rest of the orders first?" I asked. I was busily attaching pink ribbons to a special set of thank-you notes for a lady on the ninth floor.

"If we deliver these, we'll get paid for them," JBIII pointed out, but we decided to wait since it was only 9:00 and we didn't want to embarrass/annoy/wake up any of our clients.

Sunday turned out to be quite a day for us. Here's what we'd done by dinnertime:

1. Filled all the orders we had taken the day before.

2. Delivered the orders and gotten paid for them.

3. Reimbursed (which is a fancy economics word meaning "paid back") the Brubakers for their loan. (I made them tear up the contract since I didn't want a piece of paper hanging around that said JBIII and I owed anybody $$.)

4. Taken orders on floors 2–4 of JBIII's building.

5. Bought supplies for the new orders and paid for them out of our profits from the first orders. IMPORTANT NOTE: I still had some $$ left over, and I had a brand-new idea for what to do with all the cash I'd be earning.

6. Started filling the new orders.

"And just think," said JBIII happily as he set to work printing out a sheet of mouse-and-cheese address labels, "when we get paid for these orders, we'll make even more money than before because we won't have to pay my parents back for anything."

The next week was very exciting. JBIII and I took orders every morning and spent the afternoons filling them. When we ran out of people in JBIII's building we went door-to-door in my building.

"And when we're done with my building we can show our products to our parents' friends," I said. "Oh! Oh!

And we could go to The Towers and show the sample book to Daddy Bo's friends."

"My dad could take the book to his store," suggested JBIII.

We were going to be millionaires.

JBIII and I were careful with our money. We never bought more supplies than we needed and we always bought the supplies as soon as we'd gotten paid, so we didn't have to borrow any more $$. And one day we even gave $10 to the Brubakers since we were using their computer equipment so much. And they accepted it, instead of saying, like, "Oh, no, children, you hang on to this," because they knew we were running a professional outfit.

I was very busy. And happy. It was hard to believe that not long ago I'd been dragging pathetically around the house with nothing to do except make a necklace for Bitey and sing mean songs about Lexie. Now I saw JBIII every day. We took orders and filled them, and in my spare time I thought up new designs. Our sample book was growing. I wasn't rich exactly, but my wallet was getting fatter. And the days were flying by.

Which is why I was surprised when one afternoon as JBIII and I were working in his room (his mother needed the computer so we had temporarily moved our operations out of the office), my best friend said, "I can't believe the summer is over."

"It isn't over," I said automatically.

"Well, I know it isn't *technically* over. That won't happen until the end of September. But school starts in six days."

"WHAT?" I was working on a special-order card—gluing white pom-poms onto bunnies where their tails should be—and I stopped with my hands in midair.

"Yup," said JBIII. "Six days."

"But that's impossible." Hadn't I *just* been sitting in Mr. Potter's room, lying to my friends about my nonexistent trip to the Wild West?

"Nope. It really is six days."

Then it was time to carry out the idea I'd had.

That night Mom and Dad and Lexie and I ate dinner in the family room as usual. Since I was now a businessperson, earning $$ and being responsible (finally) and mature (sort of), I cleared a space for myself at Dad's desk and ate my tuna-noodle casserole without spilling a bit. Every now and then, particularly when I reached for my glass of milk, one of my family members would look at me nervously, but the meal was uneventful.

I waited until we had all finished eating and then I cleared the table. Dad stood up to help me, but I said, "No, you stay there. Let me do this. I promise I won't drop anything."

And I didn't.

This was surprising enough, but I had another surprise in store for my family. When I returned to the table

I reached into my pocket, pulled out a wad of bills, and set it on the table. The wad was so fat that when I'd tried to stuff all the $$ into my wallet a little earlier, the wallet wouldn't close.

Lexie looked at the bills and raised her eyebrows. "Where did that come from?"

"From P&J Designs," I replied, which that is what JBIII and I had named our business.

"You earned all that?" asked my sister.

"Well, more really, since JBThree and I have to buy our supplies with our earnings. And also, I wanted a yo-yo. But this is what's left over."

"Pearl, I am so proud of you!" exclaimed my mother.

"You and JB had a good idea and you carried it out very professionally," added Dad.

"Well, actually, JBThree had the original idea," I said modestly.

"But you have the artistic talent," said Mom. "And you really are treating your idea professionally."

Mom and Dad had each ordered something from P&J Designs, and they had received the finished products in a timely fashion, which had impressed them.

"Are you still getting orders?" asked Lexie, eyeing my wad again.

"Yup. Every day. We take orders in the morning and fill them in the afternoon. I guess we'll have to slow down when school starts, though. Speaking of which,"

I continued, "are we going to BuyMore-PayLess for back-to-school shopping on Saturday?"

We went there so often now that we had each been given a free green canvas SHOP HAPPY AT BUYMORE-PAYLESS! bag. We left the bags hanging on the knob of our front door so we wouldn't forget to take them with us every time we headed for the subway to Brooklyn.

Mom nodded. "I think we'd better. Saturday will be our only chance before school begins."

"Good," I said. I pushed the $$ farther across the table toward my parents. "That's for the trip."

"What?" said Mom and Dad.

"You're kidding, right?" said Lexie, and I couldn't tell whether she was surprised or jealous.

"I don't know if it will pay for everything I need," I went on, "because I kind of grew out of a lot of my clothes over the summer, but I want to pay for as much as I can."

"All your earnings? Are you sure?" said Mom, and tears filled her eyes, which is not a normal thing, in that I mostly make her cry by dropping eggs out of the window or forgetting to hand in my homework for an entire week.

"I'm sure," I said. And I was. There was just one sad thing about the success of P&J Designs, which was that now Dad was the only Littlefield without a job of his own. His wife was employed and his daughters were employed and Dad was sort of earning some $$ here and there, but it just wasn't the same as when he was the important economics professor, a job he loved and wanted back.

Two days later Mom and Dad and Lexie and I walked through the entrance of BuyMore-PayLess, each with a SHOP HAPPY bag slung over one shoulder. Mom was holding a list that was almost as long as the one she'd consulted while packing me up for my overnight week at Camp Merrimac. She glanced at it, then said, "Okay, grab two shopping carts. The list is long and the morning is short." (Sometimes I can sort of see why my mother became a writer.) She tore the list in half and handed the bottom part to my father. "We'll split up. You and Lexie go together, and I'll go with Pearl, since she might need some help trying on clothes." (Which I didn't, since I was ten, for heaven's sake, but whatever.)

"Now," Mom went on, looking around the store, which is approx. the size of an airport, "school supplies are over there, winter coats are over there, and girls' clothes are over there. We don't need any food, so we can avoid the grocery aisles. All right. Let's get going."

I looked at our half of the list as Dad and Lexie trundled away. I certainly did need a lot of things—notebooks, a new backpack, an assignment pad, a calculator, socks, underwear, sneakers, a winter jacket, jeans, a fleece top . . . I guess this is what happens when you enter fifth grade and also have a growth spurt.

"I only have forty-two dollars and eleven cents," I whispered to Mom.

"Don't forget that this is a discount store," she replied. "And there's a sale on. You'll be surprised by how far your money will go."

We walked up and down the aisles and compared prices and looked for bargains, and slowly our cart filled up and Mom crossed things off the list. An hour and a half later we met up with Dad and Lexie at the checkout line. Their cart was as full as ours. I clutched my over-stuffed wallet, and I noticed that Lexie was rummaging around in her purse. She was going to pay for some of her things, too.

We waited on a long line and I eyed an array of gum and thought of all the money in my wallet, but I turned away and just stood on one foot and then the other until at last the very loud man in front of us finished yelling at the cashier and we could finally unload our carts. To make up for the loud, rude man I said to the cashier, "We're doing our back-to-school shopping here at BuyMore-PayLess, and I'm spending forty-two dollars and eleven cents that I earned myself. Thank you for ringing us up."

The cashier smiled at me, which was good because the loud man had almost made her cry and her eyes were still full of tears that hadn't run out.

When all of our purchases had been loaded into bags, the cashier announced the price, and Lexie and I handed our money to Dad the economist and without even needing the calculator I'd just bought, he said, "You girls contributed over a quarter of the total. Thank you!"

And we all walked out of the store with our bulging shopping bags feeling pleased with ourselves.

Four nights later, which was the night before the first day of school, which also meant that it was a school night, I added the final touch to my summer scrapbook—a thank-you note, one of our P&J Designs. I had fastened a lavender ribbon to the top and a row of glitter flowers along the bottom. Inside I had written:

> Dear Mom and Dad,
> Thank you for the great summer. It was great. I really mean it. I LOVED IT! I had fun and learned a lot and also earned a lot of $$ and didn't really miss the wild west. Thank you for Camp Merrimac and our staycation and all the clothes and things from Buymore+payless, the ones you bought, not

the ones I bought. I hope you like this scrapbook. I made it just for you.

Love,

Your daughter, Pearl Littlefield

P.S. Thank you for the scrapbook too. I really mean it.

I brought the scrapbook to the family room and Mom came out of her office and Dad set aside the article he was writing and we looked through the book together, until Mom reminded me that it was a school night and I had a new bedtime schedule.

"Good night," I said, leaving the scrapbook on the coffee table because Mom said it deserved to be displayed. "Thanks again for the summer. Love you."

I found Bitey and carried him, struggling and hissing, to my bed.

One thing my parents don't usually experience is me still doing my homework at 11:00 p.m. If I'm up that late on a school night I'm either sick, or doing something I don't want anyone to know about, like drawing pictures of Mrs. Olson getting arrested for playing her flute in her nightgown and being taken to jail on the back of the policeman's bicycle.

But on the first night of fifth grade my mother knocked on my door at 11:00, peeked inside, saw me sitting at my desk surrounded by sheets of paper (which they were sheets of work, not sheets of drawings), and had to steady herself on the door frame. I couldn't blame Mom for being shocked. I rarely spend more than half an hour racing through my homework. But once I'd written Ms. Brody's outline and started filling in all the stuff she wanted to know about my summer, the words just kept spilling out, and I wrote and wrote and wrote—about Camp Merrimac and the staycation and my fight with JBIII and my father and his job search and, really, about my life (so far).

"Pearl?" said Mom. "Is that your homework?" She gasped a little.

"Yup."

"But it's eleven o'clock. When did you start it?"

"When you told me to."

"And you're still working on it? What on earth was Ms. Brody's assignment?"

I knew Mom was wondering if Ms. Brody was going to turn out to be one of those teachers who give so much homework that her students get stressed and start to fear school and also have to give up soccer. Since I already sort of liked Ms. Brody I said quickly, "Just an essay about our summer vacation. And we were supposed to outline it first."

I searched through the papers on my desk and dangled one of them in front of my mother. "This is the outline."

Mom took it and skimmed it. But she didn't comment on it. All she said was, "And what's that?" She pointed to the rest of the papers.

"The essay. I started writing and it got a little long. It's about summer vacation, but it's kind of about my life, too. I started with . . ." I paused. "I hope you don't mind, but I started with Dad getting fired. I know it's a personal family thing, but I felt like nothing that happened this summer would have happened the same way if Dad hadn't lost his job. And some of the things wouldn't have happened at all."

Once again my mother's eyes filled with tears, and once again they were not sad tears but emotional ones. "Oh, Pearl," she said, "you've discovered what it means to be a real writer—to write from your heart."

I whisked the outline from her hands and then scrabbled up all the other pages of the assignment, which was done anyway. I was just checking for spelling mistakes.

"Would you like me to look your essay over?" asked Mom.

The answer was no, which was why I had scrabbled up the papers. But I didn't want to hurt her feelings. "That's okay," I replied. "I think I did a good job. Anyway, I'm tired."

My mother looked longingly at the essay but just said, "All right. Get some sleep now. Tomorrow will be here before you know it." Then she added hurriedly, "I'm proud of you, Pearl." But she didn't say anything more about my being a real writer, which was good since if I'm a real anything, it's an artist.

Mom kissed the top of my head, closed the door to

my room, then opened it again to let Bitey in, and finally left to say good night to Lexie.

I climbed into bed with my essay, which I decided to read one final time. The main reason it had gotten so long was Dad. The more I'd written about him, the more I'd had to say. And I do not mean the more I'd had to say about missing our trip to the Wild West, although it had occurred to me that one other thing I had hoped to do out there was set up an easel in the desert and paint a sunset. I had stopped mentioning the trip because by now I knew how it felt to need a job badly and go looking for one and get turned down again and again. And if I had felt bad when no one would hire me to do something I had no business doing—like baby-sitting for someone practically my own age—imagine how Dad felt when no one would hire him to do what he was the best at, and what he loved.

I thought about P&J Designs. What if no one wanted to buy our products anymore and because of that I had to go home and tell the rest of the Littlefields that the big trip we had planned to the Wild West was cancelled? I would feel horrible. And now I knew that "horrible" meant humiliated, frustrated, embarrassed, and also that I was a failure, even though I was not. But once those feelings get going it's hard to stop them. They just roll on and on. I remembered when Dad had driven to Camp

Merrimac to watch JBIII and me in the talent showcase—the only parent who had shown up—and his sad smile as he had driven Lexie and JBIII and me home in the car he'd had to borrow from Mrs. Mott. And I remembered the look on his face when I'd held my nose on the subway, which we'd had to take since we no longer owned our green Subaru.

The loss of Dad's job hadn't just meant freezer pizza and BuyMore-PayLess and Lexie spending half her camp time as a CIT. It had meant an entire shift in my father and the way he thought about himself and the role he played in our family, and a shift in our lives.

I stared at the pages in my hands and wondered if I should add that thought somewhere or if it came through in the examples I had given Ms. Brody. I decided the examples spoke for themselves and were more interesting than plain thought-words.

I kept reading.

I reached the pages about the staycation, which was sort of a sad part since JBIII and I were having our fight then, but which mostly described a fun week. It was strange to think that you could have so much fun right in your own hometown, especially when you were supposed to be in the Wild West instead. But my family and I really had had fun, and my father had looked very happy, although who knows how he was feeling inside.

Then something else occurred to me, and it was so

important that I decided to write a P.S. at the end of the essay. I knew I was supposed to be going to sleep, but I didn't think Mom and Dad would mind if I added a finishing touch to my first fifth-grade homework assignment.

I slid out of bed and sat at my desk again. I thought for a moment and then wrote:

P.S. Ms. Brody, I know I didn't include this next part in my outline, but I didn't know where to fit it in—and I still want to add this thought to my essay, which I hope you won't take off points for not sticking 100% to the outline. Anyway, what I want to say is that I learned something important this summer, and that is that you just never know what's around the corner. And I don't mean what is really around the corner, like the time my sister and I turned off of Sixth Avenue onto Twelfth Street and almost ran into a man coming around the corner with a python around his neck and Lexie screamed and tripped and her shoe flew off.

I mean, what is coming around the corner in life. Sometimes the unexpected things are bad, like when Dad lost his job, but sometimes they're good, like when JBIII and I started our business after I had thought no one would ever hire me and I would never find a way to earn any $$. It makes me feel hopeful when I think about that. I guess what I'm trying to say is that I also feel hopeful when I think about Dad and <u>his</u> job search. Not to mention, when I think about my family and my life so far. I know I complained about my birthday party and the trip and the pizza, but still, I'm proud of my family, and that includes me, and how we worked together this summer and made changes we didn't really want to make, especially since some of the changes led to good things, like P+J Designs.

I know I'm not a writer like my mother, Ms. Brody, but I hope I've managed to explain things here. This last part seemed important.

Your student,

Pearl Littlefield, Grade 5

Now it really was time to go to bed. My head was swimming, and the words on the paper were blurring. I arranged the pages of the essay, left them on my desk, gathered Bitey into my arms, and climbed back into bed. I turned on my side and looked out my window, across the airshaft, and into a window of the building next door. A family lives in the seventh-floor apartment, a family with two parents and two little boys, and they leave one light on all night long, no matter what. I almost never see the people, just the light. It shines in a pool on their floor and on the wall by a doorway, and if I leave my blind up, it shines just a little bit into my room, too.

I looked at Bitey in the pale light from the other

apartment, and I thought about the next morning when my family and I would wake up and eat breakfast, and Lexie and I would go to school, and Mom would begin writing, and Dad would continue his search for work. One day, I thought, the phone would ring and the person at the other end would say just the thing Dad had been hoping to hear—or maybe something he hadn't expected to hear at all—and he would smile and then knock on my mother's office door to tell her the good news.

☺ PEARL'S SUMMER VACATION – OUTLINE ☺

I. My dad got fired.
  A. My family was shocked.
  B. We tried to pretend that saving $$ was fun!!!
  C. We had a tiny celebration when I hit the big one-oh.

II. I went to Camp Merrimac, which is a day camp.
  A. Lexie was a CIT for my troop.
  B. Camp was fun even though Lexie was my CIT, and even though one of the Starlettes was Jill DiNunzio.
  C. JBIII and I starred in a talent show.

III. My self-portrait (Pearl Littlefield at Ten) was in an art exhibit.

IV. I rescued Bitey (cat).

V. JBIII and I had a fight.
  A. It started at WaterWorks.
  B. It continued at the Garlic Festival.
  C. I almost made up with JBIII, but then I didn't.

VI. There was an accident.

VII. My family went on a lame staycation.
- **A.** We pretended to be tourists in our own city.
- **B.** Even though we were on vacation, I mean staycation, my sister got an idea about becoming a working girl.

VIII. My sister and I went job hunting.
- **A.** Lexie got all the jobs.
- **B.** I found out how it feels to be my father.

IX. I finally made up with JBIII.

X. JBIII and I went into business.
- **A.** JBIII got an excellent idea.
- **B.** I surprised my parents.

XI. Summer vacation ended.

Staycation Sites

Though the city isn't quite the same as the Wild West, it's full of adventures. While on staycation, Pearl and her family saw some of New York City's most famous landmarks, which attract tourists from around the world. Here's some more information about these historic sites.

EMPIRE STATE BUILDING

Completed in 1931, the Empire State Building may be New York's most famous skyscraper. Though Pearl looked for her apartment in the streets below, observation deck visitors can look into the distance and see farther. On a sunny day, observers can see all the way to New Jersey, Connecticut, Massachusetts, Pennsylvania, and Delaware. Luckily, the building has seventy-three elevators to shuttle the building's four million yearly visitors up- and downstairs. If you look at the Manhattan skyline, you might recognize the Empire State Building by its spike-like broadcast tower or its colorful lights.

www.esbnyc.com

BROOKLYN BRIDGE

Built in 1883, the Brooklyn Bridge stretches across the East River from Manhattan to Brooklyn. Cars drive on the lower levels, while people can walk or bike across the top level. It's one of the oldest suspension bridges in the country, but its

age doesn't bother the 150,000 pedestrians and cars that cross the Brooklyn Bridge every day.
http://www.history.com/topics/brooklyn-bridge

CENTRAL PARK

When New Yorkers grow tired of seeing city streets, they stroll through Central Park, which is full of creeks, ponds, and meadows, and is even the site of a castle. The park contains twenty-one playgrounds, as well as a carousel, an ice skating rink, and twenty-six softball and baseball fields. Visitors can fish, bird-watch, play sports, have picnics, or see penguins at the Central Park Zoo—all in the middle of New York City!
http://www.centralparknyc.org

STATUE OF LIBERTY

Since 1886, the Statue of Liberty has stood on a small island south of Manhattan. Liberty is quite a large lady—her mouth is three feet wide, her index finger is eight feet long, and her head is ten feet wide. Lucky visitors can stand above Lady Liberty's head and look out from her crown. From Liberty Island, you can see the skyscrapers of downtown Manhattan, and you can also see Ellis Island, where people from around the world once landed when they immigrated to America.
www.nps.gov/stli

MADAME TUSSAUDS

There are more than 200 statues of celebrities in Madame Tussauds. Visitors can take pictures with figures such as Abraham Lincoln, Marilyn Monroe, Pablo Picasso, and other artists, musicians, and politicians. Plus, they can experience creepy surprises at the live "Scream" performance and be amazed (and possibly disgusted) by the sights, sounds, and smells of their 4-D movie theater.

http://www.madametussauds.com/NewYork/

METROPOLITAN MUSEUM OF ART

At the Metropolitan Museum of Art, visitors can see everything from paintings of George Washington to ancient Greek sculptures. There is also a room furnished like a historic mansion, a hall with suits of armor, and a reconstructed Egyptian temple with a moat. It's easy to get lost while exploring the maze-like galleries.

http://www.metmuseum.org/

BROADWAY

Though Broadway is a street that winds through Manhattan, Broadway shows are put on in any of forty theaters on just a small section of Broadway near Times Square. Tourists and New Yorkers alike flock to theaters to see the many musicals and plays.

http://www.ilovenytheater.com

AMERICAN MUSEUM OF NATURAL HISTORY

The museum is famous for its dinosaur wing and its life-like animal dioramas. An ocean life wing holds models of different fish, as well as a 94-foot-long model of a blue whale. The Hayden Planetarium offers space shows which simulate the stars, planets, and universe.

http://www.amnh.org/

Thank you for reading this
FEIWEL AND FRIENDS book.
The Friends who made

TEN GOOD and BAD things About mY LIFE (So far)

possible are:

Jean Feiwel, publisher

Liz Szabla, editor-in-chief

Rich Deas, creative director

Elizabeth Fithian, marketing director

Holly West, assistant to the publisher

Dave Barrett, managing editor

Nicole Liebowitz Moulaison, production manager

Ksenia Winnicki, publishing associate

Anna Roberto, assistant editor

Find out more about our authors and
artists and our future publishing at
mackids.com.

OUR BOOKS ARE FRIENDS FOR LIFE